This is my Book

Richard Bye

HE STRAINED TO MOVE THE ROCK.

"Bomba at the Moving Mountain."　　　　　　　*Page* 150

BOMBA
THE JUNGLE BOY
AT THE MOVING
MOUNTAIN

OR

The Mystery of the Caves of Fire

BY

ROY ROCKWOOD

AUTHOR OF "BOMBA THE JUNGLE BOY," "ON A
TORN-AWAY WORLD," "LOST ON THE
MOON," ETC.

ILLUSTRATED

NEW YORK
CUPPLES & LEON COMPANY
PUBLISHERS

CONTENTS

CONTENTS

BOMBA THE JUNGLE BOY
AT THE MOVING MOUNTAIN

CHAPTER I

THE HISS OF THE SERPENT

As SILENTLY as a panther, Bomba climbed the great dolado tree, the giant of the forest.

It was a hard task, for the trunk was full of sharp-pointed spines and a thrust of one of these might mean fever and death.

But the tree was on the top of a hill and towered so far above its fellows that it would give Bomba a view of the jungle for many miles around.

Bomba needed that view, for there was trouble brewing, trouble for himself and trouble for old Cody Casson, and it behooved the boy to be on the alert, if he and his companion were to escape with whole skins.

So he went up the tree with almost the litheness and agility of Doto, his chief friend among the monkeys, climbing in the way that Doto had taught him, not by using his knees, but relying wholly on his hands and feet, the former so hardened by his jungle life that no spines could penetrate them, and the latter protected by his homemade sandals.

Deftly he made his way through the branches, until the increasing slenderness of the upper boughs warned him that they would break beneath his weight if he went any higher. Then he made himself a seat among the foliage and, drawing a deep breath, scanned the surrounding country with eyes that were almost as keen as those of a hawk.

He was a striking figure as he half-sat, half-stood there, sweeping the horizon, himself in such perfect harmony with the jungle that he seemed to be a part of it.

Bomba was a boy of about fourteen years of age, of more than medium height and so remarkably developed physically that he might easily have been supposed to be much older than he was. He had wavy brown hair, keen brown eyes, and a skin that was deeply bronzed by the heat of tropical suns. As far as color went, he might have been one of the native Indians of the Amazonian jungle; but his features showed that he was of white blood.

He wore no clothing save a breech-clout of native cotton, a pair of sandals that he himself had made, and a puma skin—the skin of Geluk, the puma, which Bomba had slain when it had tried to kill Kiki and Woowoo, the friendly parrots. The skin, held by straps at the shoulders, covered his breast and formed a partial protection against the stings of insects and the thorns of the jungle.

His arms were powerful and symmetrical, with muscles that rippled beneath the brown skin at every movement and betrayed the strength and agility that lay in them.

In his belt was thrust a machete, a knife nearly a foot in length with its two edges ground almost to razor sharpness. In addition he carried a revolver, his most precious possession and the only one he had ever owned, or even seen, the gift of white rubber hunters when he had saved their camp from an attack by jaguars, the tigers of the South American jungle. His bow and arrows he had left at the foot of the tree when he had begun his climb.

He had seen signs that day that filled him with anxiety. Enemies were abroad in the jungle. Not merely his animal foes, the jaguars, reptiles, alligators and others, against which he had constantly to be on his guard.

But the ones he had in mind at the moment were human enemies, tall, powerful, cruel-looking Indians, who, from the signs painted on their breasts and faces, he knew were on the warpath.

He had caught sight of a party of these earlier in the day, and from a secure covert in the underbrush had watched them as they had drifted along like so many shadows over a jungle trail.

At the belts of some of them hung human heads, the dreadful trophies from some onslaught upon a native village. They were the headhunters, a distant tribe living in the vicinity of the Giant Cataract, who occasionally left their native haunts on a foray against more peaceful tribes, leaving desolation and death in their wake.

Bomba had already had one experience with the headhunters, and had escaped death by the narrowest of margins. In the struggle he had wounded Nascanora, their chief. Were these men whom he had seen to-day a part of Nascanora's band, perhaps under his leadership, returning to seek vengeance? In any event, he knew them for enemies. If he should fall into their hands his life would not be worth a moment's purchase.

His first study of the jungle from his lofty perch yielded no results. The great expanse of trees and streams and underbrush was apparently destitute of all signs of human life.

But as his gaze grew more intent he caught sight of a thin wisp of smoke rising above the trees at a distance. So tenuous and slender was it that at first he was inclined to think it a shred

of vapor rising from the lush vegetation, steaming under the fierce rays of the sun.

But it had a quality in it different from that of steam, for it yielded more readily to vagrant breaths of winds, and he knew it betokened the presence of human beings.

Some one had stopped there to make a fire. It might have been a member or members of some of the more or less friendly tribes of the district, with whom, although he was not on terms of intimacy, he had no quarrel. In that case, the smoke was nothing to be viewed with concern.

But—and this was the thought that made his pulses beat more rapidly—it was far more likely that the drift of smoke indicated a temporary encampment of the dreaded headhunters. For when these ferocious invaders made their appearance in this part of the jungle, it was the signal for the native inhabitants to gather together their women and children and such property as they could carry and flee to some of the more inaccessible parts of the region, where they hid themselves until the marauders, wearied with slaughter of whomever they could find, should retire to their distant villages, bearing their hideous trophies of human heads, with which they adorned their wigwams.

Bomba strained his eyes to follow the column

of smoke from its apex to the ground, so that he might see what was going on beneath the trees.

But too much foliage intervened, and he was forced to shift his position in order to obtain a better view. This made it necessary to ascend still higher into the branches. The attempt was fraught with peril, for he had already reached the limit of safety. The branches were even now giving forth ominous chacklings as he trusted his weight to them. Should they give way, he would go crashing to the ground, nearly two hundred feet below.

But the urge of discovery was too strong to be resisted, and with the utmost wariness he worked his way upward inch by inch, distributing his weight by placing each foot on a different branch.

Then an exclamation of satisfaction broke from his lips, for he had found an opening through which he could see what he sought.

And the sight thrilled him.

In a small glade of the jungle he saw a party of stalwart Indians gathered about a fire over which strips of meat were roasting.

The men were grouped in knots on the grass, most of them eating, while others, who seemed to have finished their meal, were jabbering together excitedly.

They were of an entirely different type from

the natives near whom Bomba and Cody Casson lived, and he knew them at once for headhunters, some of them, no doubt, the very ones he had watched from his covert that morning.

But it was not upon them that his gaze rested for long. His eyes found something far more compelling beneath a group of trees on the edge of the clearing.

Tied securely to those trees were four captives. Bomba could see at a glance that they were not natives. They were white men!

He had seen only two white men in all his life, besides Cody Casson. That was on the never-to-be-forgotten day when he had met Ralph Gillis and Jake Dorn and had thrilled to the consciousness that he himself was white. He remembered how they had looked, how they had borne themselves, how they had been dressed.

These captives wore the same kind of explorers' outfits, and, despite the cords that bound them, bore the indefinable marks of a superior race.

Yes, they were white! And Bomba was white, as he had assured himself proudly every day since he had met the rubber hunters. His heart bounded with the surge of kinship that went through it. The men were his brothers!

And in what a pitiable plight! Captives of these bloodthirsty fiends of the jungle! Bomba shuddered as he thought of the terrible fate that awaited them.

His heart swelling with pity and sympathy, Bomba scanned the prisoners more closely. He could not detect their features at that distance, but one of the four caught his attention as being different from the others.

The figure was slenderer and not so tall, and a great mass of golden hair fell from the head over the shoulders. Bomba caught his breath.

He had never seen such hair, had never seen a white woman. But he knew instinctively that he saw one now. Perhaps his mother, whom he had never known, had had such hair.

A woman! And in the hands of those monsters! His blood boiled at the thought.

He must save her! He must save them all! Were they not his own kind? They were white. He was white. He felt the call of the blood.

But how could he do it alone and unaided, he a mere boy against a host of enemies?

He did not stop to answer the question. He would do that as he went along. His jungle craft and his stout heart had always helped him. He believed that they would help him now. He must not delay a moment, even to formulate a plan of action.

Without any definite idea as to what plan he would adopt, he started to descend from the tree.

Then he stopped as though he had turned to stone.

From some point near at hand he had heard a sound that chilled his blood.

It was the hiss of a jaracara, one of the deadliest snakes of the Amazonian jungle!

At the sound of that sibilant hiss, Bomba's heart seemed to stand still for a moment. He was at no loss to grasp the sinister portent.

The deadly snake was close at hand, in the same tree as himself. And what was more, the sound came from below. The snake was between him and the ground!

CHAPTER II

IN DEADLY PERIL

THE boy could climb no higher. He was already at the extreme limit of safety. And even if he could ascend, the snake would follow him.

Bomba looked wildly about at the adjoining trees. But there was no hope there. The branches of the nearest one were nearly thirty feet away. Even a monkey could not have made the leap.

Again came that terrible hiss, this time nearer. The snake was crawling toward him. But the thick foliage below had thus far hidden it from sight.

Now Bomba could hear the rustling of the leaves as the slimy monster wound its way among them. Death was coming toward him!

Bomba's hand sought the revolver at his belt. But the hand stopped before it reached the weapon, for he remembered the savages. The report of the weapon would bring them whooping to the tree and they would have five captives instead of four. And as between the human and reptile enemies, Bomba preferred to take his chance with the snake.

As he reached this conclusion, his eye was caught by a movement on a bough below. The leaves were rising and lowering in horrid undulations, as a long writhing body made its way among them, coming in his direction.

Then suddenly a cluster of leaves parted, and a wicked triangular head appeared, rising slowly from a long black neck, while two malignant eyes with a fiendish glint in them fastened themselves upon the lad.

Like a flash, Bomba drew his knife and braced himself for battle.

While the boy stands at bay, his eyes fixed upon the awful head and slavering jaws drawing nearer with the relentlessness of doom, it may be well for the benefit of those who have not read the preceding volume of this series to tell who Bomba was and something of his adventures up to the time this story opens.

As far back as Bomba could remember he had dwelt in the depths of the jungle. His only companion had been Cody Casson, an aged naturalist, whether related to him or not, Bomba did not know.

The boy had grown up in absolute ignorance of the world at large. His only world was the

jungle, but with this he was thoroughly familiar,
He knew every bird and animal and reptile in it,
their lairs and haunts and habits. Some of the
more harmless ones, such as the parrots and the
monkeys, were his friends. He understood their
gestures and their language, and their company
was a relief to the loneliness that at times over-
whelmed him.

Neither he nor Casson had much to do with the
natives of that part of the jungle, who, though
not hostile, held aloft from a superstitious feeling that the white man practised magic and might
do them evil if he were so inclined.

The old naturalist had given Bomba some
smattering of education. But this had not gone
far, for the explosion of a rifle that Casson had
fired at an anaconda that was attacking Bomba
had injured the old man's head and made him
childish. From that time the lessons had ceased,
and the care of providing food for the two had
devolved on Bomba.

The danger involved in this had developed the
boy into a mighty hunter, a dead shot with bow
and arrow, a master of the spear and the machete,
quick, crafty and resourceful, a match for any of
the deadly inhabitants of the jungle.

But Bomba was lonely, restless, and unhappy.
He knew that he was out of place in the jungle.
He was different from the natives. His white

blood and instincts called him elsewhere. He was in a turmoil of longing for he knew not what.

An accidental meeting with two white rubber hunters, whose lives he saved when their camp was attacked by jaguars, had intensified these longings. They had wanted him to go with them to civilization, but he could not leave Casson.

He had besought the latter to tell him something of his parents, and the old naturalist had tried to do so. But his memory had failed him. He had spoken vaguely of "Bartow" and "Laura," persons whom Bomba finally guessed must be connected in some way with his history.

What exciting adventures Bomba had with boa constrictors, jaguars and alligators, how narrowly he escaped death from vampires, the way he saved his monkey friends from the attack of the vultures, the desperate and successful defense of his cabin against the hordes of Nascanora—these and other exploits are narrated in the preceding volume of this series, entitled: "Bomba the Jungle Boy; or, The Old Naturalist's Secret."

Now to return to Bomba as he stands in the topmost branches of the tree, knife in hand, facing the scaly monster that seeks his life.

The snake was coming more slowly now. It saw the tense attitude of its intended victim, noted the knife in his hand, and knew that a struggle was impending.

But there was no relaxation of its purpose. Its forked tongue darted between the thin lips that were like a gash in the horrible face.

Bomba realized that victory would go to the one that was the quicker of the two. The snake would strike like lightning. He must try to parry with his knife and slice the snake in two. There was little chance to dodge. There was absolutely no chance to retreat.

Bomba knew that the chances were against him. Deft and agile as he was, the snake was quicker.

Nearer and nearer came the reptile, measuring the distance. Eight feet away—seven—six. There the reptile stopped to throw itself into the coil from which it would launch the deadly stroke.

And in that moment an inspiration came to Bomba.

He caught hold of the end of the bough the snake had been ascending, bent it down as far as he could with all the strength of his muscular arms, and then released it.

The tough, elastic bough shot upward against the one just above it, catching the body of the snake between the two. The force of the impact drove the sharp spines into the reptile from above and below, holding it impaled.

There was a fearful hissing and writhing as the

monster thrashed about, trying to release itself.
But it was held as between the jaws of a trap.

It bit and tore at the stabbing spines furiously,
but its struggles only served to drive them deeper.
Then it turned and struck out savagely again and
again at Bomba. But stretch and strain as it
would, the strokes fell two feet short, though the
poison expelled from its fangs spattered against
the puma skin that covered the boy's breast.

Repeatedly it tried until its strength was exhausted. Then Bomba, watching his opportunity,
lunged forward as the neck fell limp and severed
the snake's head from its body.

The head fell through the tree to the ground,
though several minutes elapsed before the writhing of the folds ceased.

Bomba wiped his knife on the leaves and re-
stored it to its place in his belt. His heart was
beating with excitement, but his nerves were tingling with exultation. Once more that wily brain of
his had extricated him from a plight that had
seemed to mean certain death.

But he could not stop long to indulge in re-
joicing. He knew that these terrible reptiles usu-
ally traveled in pairs and the mate of the one he
had killed was probably not far off. It might be
in that very tree.

But before Bomba began his descent, he cast
one more look abroad from his lofty perch.

The group of white people in the glade were as he had seen them. But the meal now seemed to be over and the savages had risen from their sprawling postures on the grass and were gathered together in animated council.

Leaving them for a moment, Bomba's eyes swept the horizon, and his heart gave a bound as he detected the smoke from another camp-fire in a different direction.

This second column was in the vicinity of the cabin in which Bomba made his home with Casson! Poor old Casson, weak and sick and bewildered in mind! What chance would he have, if he were attacked by the headhunters? Not the least in the world, thought Bomba, his heart turning sick with apprehension.

He must get to the old naturalist at once. If he could not live with Casson, he could at least die with him.

Moving with the utmost celerity, but keeping his eyes open for any stirring of the foliage that might betray the presence of the mate of the dead reptile, the boy made his way down the tree to the ground.

He reached it in safety, gathered up his bow and arrows, and with a look of disgust and repulsion at the grinning head that lay there, the jaws still open but the eyes glazed in death, started in the direction of the cabin.

It was here that his first duty lay. It gave him a wrench to abandon his resolution of helping the captives, especially the woman, whose plight had so deeply stirred him to pity. But this task had to be postponed. He must save Casson first. If he succeeded in this, he promised himself to take up the trail later and do what he could for the others.

As he traversed the jungle some of his animal friends saw and joined him. Kiki and Woowoo, the parrots, swooped down upon him, one on each shoulder, chattering and rubbing their heads against his. Doto, the monkey, dropped down from a tree and ambled along by his side, telling him in simian language how glad he was to see him.

At almost any other time Bomba would have stopped to talk and play with them, but now he was too worried and intent upon his errand to do more than give them a hasty caress and tell them that his heart was sad and burdened and that he must hurry on. They sensed his absorption, and one by one withdrew, though he was conscious that they were accompanying him overhead.

Bomba tore along at a rapid pace until he knew that he was near the place where he had seen the second column of smoke. Then he relaxed his speed, and moved forward with the stealth of a panther.

A little later he sniffed the smoke of a campfire and heard a jabber of voices.

Instantly he dropped to the ground and wormed his way on his stomach through the thick underbrush until he came to a spot where, by cautiously peering through the leaves, he could see a score or more of savages, whom he knew to be headhunters.

They had evidently just concluded their meal and were gathering their weapons together in preparation for moving on.

Bomba glanced from one to another of the faces in search of Nascanora, his bitterest enemy. But Nascanora was not there. The man who seemed to be chief, judging by the deference shown him by the others, was as tall and powerful as Nascanora and bore some resemblance to him.

Bomba recalled what Hondura, a friendly native chief, one time had told him, that Nascanora had a half-brother, Tocarora by name, with whom he divided the chieftainship of the tribe. It might very well be, thought Bomba, that the leader he now looked upon was Tocarora, come perhaps to avenge the wound that Bomba had inflicted upon his brother the night the headhunters had attacked his and Casson's cabin.

One fact especially made this seem probable. Hondura had told things that made Bomba believe that Tocarora was at times half-crazy, owing to a blow that he had received in a fight. Bomba thought that now he could see in the leader's eyes a lurid light that bespoke a deranged mind.

But the boy had little time to spend in speculation. The savages were preparing to march, and, from the gestures of the chief, they intended to go in the direction of the cabin. At all costs, Bomba must get there first.

He made a circuit of the camp, and when he was confident that he was out of sight and earshot, rose to his feet and made for the hut with the swiftness of a deer.

Roots reached out to trip him up, long vines depending from the trees sought to throttle him, the underbrush tugged at him as he forced his way through. But he kept on, summoning all his speed and strength, until finally he broke into the little clearing where the cabin lay.

The door was ajar, and he rushed into the hut, where Casson was lying asleep in his hammock.

The sudden incursion roused the old man, and he started up in alarm.

He was so frail that it seemed as though a breath would blow him away. Straggling locks of white hair formed a frame for a face as withered and colorless as parchment. The lines in his face had been graven there by intellect and force of character, but there was no indication now of either of these qualities in the faded blue eyes that were turned on Bomba.

"What is the matter?"

"The headhunters!" panted Bomba. "They are coming! They will try to kill us!"

"The headhunters!" exclaimed Casson incredulously. "How do you know?"

"I saw them," cried Bomba. "Do not talk. Do not wait. We must go. We must hide. Quick!"

He half lifted the stupefied old man from the hammock and set him on his feet. Then he darted about the cabin, replenishing his stock of cartridges and arrows and gathering up what food he could find.

An exclamation from Casson caused Bomba to whirl about. His heart sank as he looked through the doorway into the open.

A swarm of savages was pouring from the jungle and rushing toward the hut!

CHAPTER III

THE WHITE MAN'S MAGIC

LIKE a flash Bomba darted to the door, slammed it shut, and dropped the heavy bar into place.

He was not a moment too soon, for the next instant there came the impact of heavy bodies against the door. But the bar held, and the assailants fell back to the fringe of the forest, where, concealed by the trees, they could deliberate upon their next move, now that their attempt to spring a surprise had failed.

After all, they had plenty of time. Their quarry was trapped and could not escape. The appearance of either one outside the door would be the signal for his being shot full of arrows before he could go ten feet.

Although despair tugged at Bomba's heart, he gave no indication of it. The instant he had slipped the bar into place he began making his preparations for defence. The five chambers of his revolver were loaded and a supply of cartridges lay near by. A sheaf of arrows was placed close to his hand. Seated by one of the loopholes with which he had provided the cabin, he looked toward the woods for a target. None presented itself, and his little store of ammunition did not permit him to engage in aimless shooting.

The woods beyond remained as silent as the grave. Bomba wondered how long that calm would continue. He glanced at the position of the sun and saw that it was about the middle of the afternoon. He thought it possible that the savages would defer their main attack until after dark. It was likely, too, that they were waiting for others of their party—those, perhaps, who had captured the whites—to rejoin them so that they might be in full force when they made their final assault.

Still, it was surprising, considering their immense advantage in numbers, that they did not attack at once. Bomba smiled to himself grimly as he guessed the reason. The little garrison was held in wholesome respect. The savages remembered all too well what had happened to others of their tribe on a previous occasion such as this and were not at all desirous of taking any chances that might be avoided.

Casson, who at first had been stupefied by Bomba's sudden irruption with his startling news, now regained something of self-possession and joined with Bomba as well as he could in the preparations for defence.

When all was done that could be done, the old man crept close to Bomba where he was maintaining his vigil.

"Is it Nascanora who has come back?" he asked.

"No," replied Bomba. "Nascanora is not with them. He was hurt the last time he came, and now he may be dead. Or he may be with another part of the tribe," and he went on to narrate what he had seen of the savages and their captives from the top of the dolado tree.

The old naturalist sighed heavily.

"Heaven help those poor creatures if they are in the hands of the headhunters!" he murmured.

"Who is heaven and how can he help them?" asked Bomba, with his usual directness.

But Casson made no answer. He seemed to be deep in cogitation.

"Who was the leader of the party that you saw?" he asked, after a long silence.

"He was a man who looked like Nascanora, but his eyes were strange," replied Bomba. "I think it was Tocarora, the man whose mind is not right, the one who, from what Hondura says, is a half-crazy man."

At this moment there came a long, curious cry from the trees behind which the savages were hidden. It was not a war whoop, but seemed designed to attract the attention of the besieged.

A moment later it was repeated, and then a voice came from some unseen speaker.

"Tocarora would make talk with the white man," said the voice.

Bomba and Casson looked at each other.

"What shall we do?" asked Bomba.

"We will listen to him," replied Casson. "It will do no harm. Your voice is stronger than mine. Call out to him that we will hear his talk, but he must come out where we can see him, so that we may know we are talking to a chief who will be able to do what he says he will do."

Bomba repeated the message, using the speech common to the natives of the jungle, that which, with some slight variations, could be understood by all the tribes.

There was a pause, probably for consultation, and then an answer came back.

"If the white man will not shoot with his arrows or the iron stick that spits fire, Tocarora will come," the voice said. "And the white man too must come out to meet him."

The proposition was fair enough, if no thought of treachery lay behind it. But concerning this Bomba was very dubious. He looked doubtfully at Casson.

To his surprise a great transformation had

taken place in the appearance of the old naturalist. He was under the influence of some idea that seemed to have electrified him. His apathy had given place to energy. For the moment he was the keen alert scientist whom Bomba had known before the accident that had robbed him of his memory.

"Tell him yes," he said to Bomba, who was staring at him as though he could not believe his eyes; "but tell him that if his tongue is forked, the fire stick will speak and he will die. He must come without weapons, and must tell his men not to shoot. I will do the same. When the talk is over, he may go back unhurt to his men and I will come back to the cabin."

Bomba repeated the directions, although he was by no means convinced of their wisdom. He had no faith in the outcome of the conference. He dreaded treachery and feared lest the simple-minded Casson should be overmatched by the cunning of the savage. He would have much preferred to carry on the parley himself.

But on the other hand he could not divest himself of the weapons, which he alone was qualified to use effectively. With these he must cover the chief during the conference and be ready to use them on the first sign of violence or bad faith.

While Bomba was relaying the message Casson moved about the hut, gathering together with feverish haste some small objects which, in the semi-darkness, Bomba could not clearly discern.

A few minutes later Tocarora stepped out from behind a tree, wholly unarmed, his hands held high above his head with the palms extended toward the cabin in sign of amity. At the same moment the door of the cabin opened and Casson stepped out, making the same amicable gestures.

They eyed each other for a brief space and then moved slowly toward each other until they stood face to face in the middle of the clearing.

They presented a striking contrast—the powerful, copper-colored savage and the frail, attenuated white man. It seemed as though the former could have broken the latter between his thumb and forefinger.

Yet there was an indefinable something that stamped Casson as the master of the situation. What was it, Bomba asked himself, that gave Casson the supremacy? And he answered his own question with a throb of exultation.

It was because Casson was white. His soul was awake. And Tocarora was a savage. His soul was asleep.

And he, Bomba, was white! He could have shouted with joy, despite the gravity of the situation.

Of the two antagonists as they faced each other, Casson was the first to speak.

"Why has Tocarora come from the Giant Cataract to the cabin of the white man?" he asked gravely.

"There is good hunting in this part of the jungle," replied Tocarora evasively.

"Tocarora speaks with a double tongue," Casson said reproachfully. "It is not well. It is not the tapir nor the jaboty that Tocarora is hunting when he rushes to the cabin of the white man and tries to get into the door."

The savage chieftain looked confused.

"There is no evil in the heart of Tocarora for the white man," he professed, though he could not meet the steady gaze of Casson's eyes. "He wants the white man to come with him to the Giant Cataract, but he will not do him harm."

"Why should I come to the Giant Cataract?" asked Casson.

"It is the will of Nascanora," replied Tocarora. "He has been ill, and many of his people have suffered from the sickness. He thinks that the white man's magic has done this, and he wants that you should remove the spell that you have laid on the tribe."

"I have laid no spell," declared Casson. "My magic is good magic. I have done no evil to Nascanora and his people. I would rather do them good."

"But it is Nascanora's will that you should

come," persisted Tocarora stubbornly. "He will make you many gifts, much cattle."

"The white man needs no gifts," said Casson haughtily. "What would my magic be worth if it did not bring me what I want? Things come to me when I call. Behold!"

From his left hand he let drop some nails and fragments of arrowheads.

"They will come to me when I call," he announced.

He bent down and extended his right hand, in the palm of which he held a magnet concealed.

"Come!" he called.

The bits of iron leaped from the ground to his hand. Casson straightened up and nonchalantly dropped them, together with the magnet into his pocket.

"What do I need of the gifts of Nascanora when even the hard iron obeys me?" he demanded.

The effect on Tocarora was prodigious. How could he doubt what he had seen with his own eyes?

He started back, his eyes bulging and the sweat of terror breaking from his face.

"The white man's magic is strong," he managed to get out from his trembling lips.

"Oh," said Casson with a gesture of indifference, "that is but little compared with what the

white man can do. He carries fire at the end of
his fingers. Behold!"

He lighted with a match a small torch of pitch
pine that he had brought with him. Tocarora
jumped as the match blazed up. He had never
seen anything like it. He viewed the stump of the
match fearfully and seemed relieved when Casson
threw it away.

Still, though this was a new method of making
fire and he did not understand it, it hardly ap-
pealed to him as supernatural.

"Tocarora make fire with stick too," he said,
referring to the native method of twirling a hard
stick in a bowl until a spark was produced.

"Yes," assented Casson, who had been busy
shuffling his feet, "but not with finger. Look!"

He blew out the torch, from which a slender
shred of smoke ran upward. Then, touching the
top of the smoke column with the tip of his finger,
now full of electricity, the torch again burst into
flame.

Tocarora's face was a study in bewilderment
and apprehension. He looked about him as
though seeking a path of retreat from the white
wonder-worker.

Casson noted the effect produced and followed
it up immediately.

"Why is Tocarora carrying betel nuts in his

ears?" he queried. "Are they a present for the white man?"

The savage put his hands impulsively to his ears.

"I have no betel nuts there," he said. "Is the white man making a mock of Tocarora?" and he drew back his lips in a menacing snarl.

Casson reached over and plucked a betel nut from Tocarora's right ear. Then he took another from his left ear. Then he plucked them in rapid succession from the savage's nose, lips, eyes and throat.

CHAPTER IV

THE IMPENDING STORM

TOCARORA staggered back, trembling and terrified, before this illustration of the white man's magic. His untutored mind had received a blow that made it reel.

He knew that he had brought no betel nuts with him. Yet here they were, plucked with nonchalance from every organ of his head.

It must be the work of demons, allies of the white man. It behooved him to go very slowly in dealing with this wonderful magician.

Casson yawned and slipped the betel nuts indifferently into his pocket.

"You see, Tocarora, it is not well to try to harm the white man," he said. "Go back to Nascanora and tell him what you have seen. Tell him that Casson has no evil in his mind toward him or his people and that he will put no spell on him if he be left alone. But if he rouses the wrath of the white man, it will be very bad for Nascanora. Will you tell him this?"

"I will tell him," mumbled Tocarora, thoroughly cowed for the moment and feeling furtively of his nose and ears.

"It is well," said Casson impressively. "And now," he added haughtily, "depart to your people and leave me alone with my slave. I have spoken."

He turned and made his way slowly to the cabin, while Tocarora made haste to seek the shelter of the woods, a far less truculent chieftain than he had been when he had emerged from them.

Casson maintained his stately attitude until he had slammed the door of the hut behind him. Then the temporary strength that he had summoned for a great emergency deserted him, and he sank, weary and exhausted, to the floor.

Bomba's mind was in a whirl. He had watched breathlessly from his loophole the course of the conference. He had been stricken with wonder almost equal to Tocarora's own at the exploits of Casson. Never had the old man shown him any of these tricks. What miracle was it that had transformed the aged naturalist into a masterful wonder worker? He felt a strange humility and an added respect for his white-haired companion, whom he had come to regard almost as a child.

"Tocarora was frightened," remarked Bomba. "He thinks you are a great magic man. And so do I. It was wonderful to see what you did. How did you do it? Was it the heaven you were speaking about that helped you?"

"Perhaps you are nearer the truth than you think," said Casson, with a faint smile, "for if anyone ever needed the help of heaven it is ourselves. But there was no magic about it. Many years ago I learned those tricks for my own amusement. I practised them till I could do them perfectly. Some day I will show you how they are done. But just now I am very tired. I must rest."

"I will help you to get into your hammock," said Bomba, rising to suit the action to the word. "You have done more with your tricks than I could do with my arrows and the fire stick. I think Tocarora and his men are so frightened at your magic that they will go away."

But Casson shook his head.

"I do not think so," he said. "They have come too far to give up their plans. Tocarora will talk to his medicine man and his headmen, and they will urge him to kill or capture us. Their squaws would laugh at them if they went back to the Giant Cataract and told them that they, although so many, were afraid of one old man and a boy. The effect of the tricks will wear off after a while, and Tocarora will be angry at himself for showing fear where his braves could see him. No, they will come again. But it will not be for a long time, maybe, not until to-morrow, for they will make long talk before they make up their minds what to do. We have given them much to think about."

The reaction was on Cody Casson now, and he was so limp and weak that Bomba had to lift him into his hammock, where he sank at once into what resembled a stupor more than a sleep.

It was with a strange medley of emotions that Bomba went back to the loophole and resumed his watch. He had been accustomed for so long to take the lead in everything that required courage and initiative that the sudden flaring up of those qualities in Casson filled him with surprise and hope. Instead of a burden, the aged naturalist had become an ally.

This meant much as a reinforcement. But might it not mean more in another direction? If Casson's memory, which had seemed dormant for years, could come back to him so that he could remember and practise tricks that had long been forgotten, why might it not recall also the facts concerning Bomba's birth and parentage that the old man had tried vainly to tell him? Why might it not explain the mysteries connected with "Bartow" and "Laura?"

Bomba's heart leaped at the possibility and he

determined to question **Casson** the moment he awoke.

But he did not permit the thoughts that thronged him to abate his vigilance by a single jot. His eyes were fastened on the fringe of trees beyond which lay his enemies.

As far as any sound was concerned, they might already have decamped. The jungle lay silent in the baking rays of the sun. No skulking figure appeared among the trees.

But Bomba permitted himself to indulge in no illusions. He knew how shadowlike could be the movements of his foes when they so desired. He did not doubt that at that very moment scores of eyes were watching him intently, ready to thwart any movement toward escape.

One reflection brought him some comfort. His enemies had not surrounded the cabin. So far as he knew, they were all in front of him. But he had little doubt that as soon as darkness came the enveloping movement would be completed.

He thought of the bark canoe hidden in a thick clump of grass on the border of the river that ran back of the hut. Ever since the previous attack he had kept a stock of dried provisions in the boat, in preparation for a hasty escape down the river. It was this he had had in mind when he had hastened through the jungle to warn Casson. But the arrival of Tocarora and his band sooner than he had expected had cut off that avenue of retreat.

The long afternoon wore on, and the evening shadows were gathering when a movement in the hammock indicated that Casson was awaking.

"Where are you, Bomba?" came in a faltering voice.

"I am here, Casson," replied the lad. "I am keeping watch against the savages."

"The savages?" repeated Casson dazedly. "What savages? Where are they?"

"Tocarora and his people," replied Bomba, his heart sinking as he realized that Casson was again groping in the land of shadows. "The man you were talking to this afternoon. The man you frightened with your tricks."

"Tricks?" muttered Casson bewilderedly.

"Yes," replied Bomba. "Don't you remember? You called to the iron and it came. You touched the smoke with your finger and the torch was lighted. You took betel nuts from his eyes and ears and mouth."

"I used to do those things," murmured Casson. "It was many, many years ago. I do not think I could do them now."

All the hopes that Bomba had nurtured collapsed like a house of cards. A great emergency had swung open the door of Casson's memory, and during that period of exaltation and reve-

lation he had been his old self.   Now the door
had swung shut again, and he was again the weak
and helpless invalid that he had become in recent
years.

Where now were Bomba's dreams of learning
what concerned him most—the meaning of "Bartow" and "Laura?"   The door was shut!

He realized this with a pang that stabbed
his heart.   But he had no time to indulge in vain
regrets.

"Listen, Casson," he said.   "The headhunters
are here only a few feet away in the jungle.
Tocarora is leading them.   You talked to him
this afternoon.   He said he wanted you to go
with him to the Giant Cataract to take the spell
off his people."

"Yes," replied Casson, rubbing his hand over
his forehead.   "I remember that now.   And I
said that I would not go."

"That is right," rejoined Bomba.   "And he
said that he would give your message to Nascanora.   But I think his tongue is forked and his
heart is black.   When the night comes, he and
his people may try to capture us or kill us.   We
must try to get away from here."

"Yes," assented Casson.   "But how?"

"I do not know yet," replied Bomba.   "We may
be able to get to the boat, or, if not, we may have

to go into the jungle. The moon will not come up till late, and we must go before it comes. We will eat now, and then carry away with us all the food we can. See, it is getting dark already."

Casson moved about submissively, doing as directed. All the fire and spirit that had marked him in his interview with Tocarora had vanished, and he was again nothing but a weak and broken old man.

Bomba noted not only that the sky was darkening, but that the wind was rising. It came in a gentle soughing at first, followed by strong gusts that steadily increased in violence.

His heart leaped as he read the signs. A tropical storm was brewing. Nature was coming to their aid!

His chief fear had been that when darkness came the savages would attempt to set fire to the cabin by shooting into the logs arrows tipped with flame. Against such an attack he would have no adequate defense.

But now, if the rain fell, the cabin would be drenched and fire could gain no foothold.

Then, too, in the pitch darkness and descending torrents their chances of escape would be redoubled. Even the keen eyes of their enemies might be baffled, and if the fugitives could once get away from the vicinity of the cabin the rain would wash away all traces of their footprints and foil the human bloodhounds that would try to follow them.

In the gathering darkness he and Casson munched the farina and cured meat, of which there was abundance in the cabin. They ate heartily in preparation for the famine that might menace them in the days to come.

Soon the very darkness seemed to grow blacker when the rain that long had threatened began to fall.

It came at first in spattering gusts that soon became torrents that beat upon the roof like thunder until it seemed that all the windows of heaven had been opened to release their floods of water.

The two within the cabin gathered up their weapons and their food supplies. Then, at a propitious moment, Bomba touched Casson on the arm.

"Come!" he said.

CHAPTER V

THE LIGHTNING STRIKES

BOMBA silently removed the heavy bar from the door.

Inch by inch he let the door swing open, standing at one side to avoid the flight of arrows he was sure would come if the movement were detected.

But no arrows came. The night outside was so dark that almost it could be felt. Bomba could not see his hand before his face. And the terrific roar of the tempest effectually prevented all other sounds from being heard.

Touching Casson's arm as a signal to follow, Bomba stepped forth and edged along the wall of the hut, making his way toward a thicket that grew at the edge of the clearing farthest from the spot where he supposed his foes to be gathered.

Once in that clump of bushes, he believed there would be little difficulty in shaping his course for the boat that seemed to offer the best chance for

40

safety. The water left no trace, and the Indians, far from home, had no craft in which they could follow, even if they suspected the course that the fugitives had taken.

The fugitives reached the thicket without discovery and had scarcely ensconced themselves in its dripping depths before a jagged shaft of lightning split the sky and made all the surroundings as bright as noonday. Had it come an instant sooner, nothing could have saved them from discovery.

Their escape had been of the narrowest. But while it had been a godsend to the fugitives, the flash also revealed something that filled Bomba with consternation.

In that moment of blinding light his eyes had detected groups of Indians scattered at short intervals between him and the boat. It was evident that as soon as darkness had come they had surrounded the cabin. Probably they had not discovered the boat, which had been securely hidden. But their presence in that locality made it impossible to reach the craft.

Their most promising method of escape had been cut off. There was no recourse now left but the jungle—the jungle that they knew to be swarming with enemies, animal and human.

Had Bomba been alone, the prospect would have held little terror for him. His keenness of eye, lightness of foot, quickness of brain, and stoutness of heart had brought him safely through so far, and he had learned to rely on them with confidence.

But with Casson, poor, old, tottering Casson, to look after and defend, the problem was a staggering one.

But Bomba and despair were strangers, and after the first shock the boy girded himself for the coming struggle.

There was another dazzling flash of lightning, followed by a terrific peal of thunder, and with the thunder was blended another roar, as a great tree, struck by the lightning bolt, wavered for a moment on the edge of the clearing and then fell forward, striking one edge of the cabin with a frightful crash.

That part of the hut was smashed into fragments. But the tree had claimed more than an inanimate victim, for with the roar of its fall came shrieks of pain and terror that told of natives buried beneath the trunk and branches.

There was a rush from the surrounding forest of the unhurt savages coming to the aid of their comrades. They worked frantically to release those whose cries told that they still lived, and Bomba noted several who were taken out from the mass and carried back into the jungle. But he also saw other silent forms that in all probability would never move again. He shuddered as he thought that, if he and Casson had stayed but a few minutes longer, they too might have been crushed to death.

He took advantage of the confusion to draw his companion after him still deeper into the jungle, where there was less chance of the lightning revealing their hiding place. There they cowered low and waited developments.

"What has happened, Bomba?" asked Casson, who in his dazed state had not grasped the meaning of the uproar.

"A tree fell on the hut," replied Bomba. "It smashed part of it and hurt many of Tocarora's people. Some of them were killed. We got out just in time."

"Perhaps they think that we were killed too," suggested Casson.

This had not struck Bomba before, and it gave him food for thought. The savages might readily suppose that the whites had been caught in the crash. They could not move the mighty tree and search in the débris of the ruined hut to make sure that their enemies had not been killed.

If this idea once got possession of them, they might go away and report to Nascanora that his vengeance had been accomplished.

But it was too early yet to hug that hope to his heart, and for at least two hours longer he and

Casson crouched in the underbrush, waiting for the next move on the part of their enemies.

By that time the tempest had spent its force. Both of the fugitives were drenched. This meant little to Bomba except discomfort, but he dreaded the effect the exposure might have upon Casson, whose hold on life, never very strong, had been still further weakened by the strain of the last few hours.

He took off his puma skin and wrapped it about the head and shoulders of the old naturalist, who was muttering as though his mind were wandering.

Listening intently, Bomba heard the heavy tread of the savages, made the heavier by the burden of their injured comrades whom the well were bearing along with them. The survivors were in an ugly mood at the miscarrying of their plans when they had seemed to have their quarry securely within their power.

They were coming nearer and nearer, and Bomba put his hand on his revolver, not knowing at what moment he might be called upon to use it.

But before they reached the thicket in which Bomba and Casson had taken refuge, the party stopped and laid down their burdens. Bomba feared that they were about to make a fire, in which event his and Casson's presence would almost certainly be revealed. But he dismissed this fear the next moment, as he reflected that after the drenching the jungle had received it would be impossible to find wood dry enough to burn.

The rain had ceased now, and the moon was beginning to peep from behind the ragged edges of the clouds. The pale light flickering between the trees enabled Bomba to see dimly the shadowy figures of his enemies as they squatted sullenly on their haunches. Only two remained standing. One of them from his height Bomba identified as Tocarora. The other, from his grotesque regalia, Bomba knew must be the medicine man of the tribe.

Bomba could see that Tocarora was nursing a wounded wrist that seemed to be giving him great pain. It had been put up roughly in splints and held in place by a bandage that went over the chief's shoulder.

The lad jumped at once to the conclusion that Tocarora had been among those who had been standing guard between the hut and the river, and this was confirmed by the growling complaint that the chief was making to the medicine man.

"Ruspak's medicine is no good," fretted Tocarora, as he looked malevolently at the priest. "Why did he not know that the tree was about to fall and warn Tocarora?"

"I told you that there was going to be thunder and lightning," Ruspak defended himself. "Tocarora knows that the lightning sometimes makes the trees go down. He should have stood further back from the hut."

"The tree fell by the white man's magic," snarled Tocarora. "He is a greater medicine man than Ruspak."

"He is not!" declared Ruspak, stung by the aspersion on his powers. "The voice of the gods speaks through me, and it would be well that Tocarora should remember that."

There was a covert threat in the last words, but the chief was too angry to desist from speech.

"I say that the white man has better medicine," he reiterated. "Can Ruspak make the iron leap to his hand? Can he light a torch by holding his finger over it? Can he take betel nuts from my eyes and ears?"

There was a murmur from the others which showed how deeply they, too, had been impressed by Casson's performances, and Ruspak turned on them in a passion.

"Dogs!" he cried, venting on them the anger that he did not quite dare to display toward their chief. "Do you dare to make a mock of Ruspak? Do you want me to call down a curse on you and your wives and children? Beware how you rouse the wrath of the messenger of the gods!"

There was an uneasy rustling among the savages, and they turned away their faces so that they might not meet the medicine man's blazing eyes.

Content with the impression made, Ruspak turned once more toward Tocarora.

"What the white man did were tricks," he declared. "I could do still greater ones if our gods were willing. Besides, if the white man's magic is so strong, why was he not able to save himself and the boy he called his slave? He could not keep the tree from falling on his own house and crushing him and his slave to death."

There seemed to be point to this argument, and the murmurs of assent showed Ruspak that he had scored with his hearers. Even Tocarora abated something of his truculence.

"It may be as you say," he said placatingly. "But if the white man is dead, why should we tarry here? Perhaps his ghost will still be strong in magic."

His hearers looked about uneasily, and their superstitious fears almost threw them into a panic when Bomba gave vent to a weird wailing moan that resounded eerily through the jungle. Tocarora was quite as startled as the rest at this apparent confirmation of his conjecture.

"The place is bad," he said with decision. "We will go from here before more harm befall us. We will tell Nascanora that the white man is dead, and he will be content."

"But not so content as if we brought back the white man's head," protested Ruspak. "Let us wait till daylight comes. We will then search for the bodies of the white man and his slave and cut off their heads. Nascanora will smile when he sees them on top of his wigwam. He will know then that we speak truth when we tell him that the Man of Evil is dead."

CHAPTER VI

CAPTURING THE SORCERER

LEST the force of Ruspak's arguments should prevail, Bomba once more emitted an uncanny moan that caused all the Indians to cluster closer together for mutual support.

"There is some wisdom in what Ruspak says," conceded Tocarora. "But there is more wisdom still in getting away from this place, which seems to rest under the curse of the gods. We will go."

Ruspak opened his mouth as though to combat this decision, but a glance about the circle convinced him that Tocarora had expressed the opinion of his followers. So with an angry shrug he submitted to the will of the majority and stalked along sullenly as the men again took up their burdens and moved away through the jungle.

Bomba's heart beat high with exultation as the sound of their footsteps finally died away in the distance. He waited until he was certain that they were out of earshot, and then turned toward Casson.

"Come, Casson," he said, as he gently shook his companion. "The headhunters are gone, and I do not think they will come back. It is safe now to go to the cabin. Come!"

But there was no response. Bomba raised the old man to a sitting position and himself arose to his feet. But as he turned to aid Casson, the latter sank back as though dead.

"Casson! Casson!" cried Bomba in alarm, as he put his arms under the old man's shoulders. "Wake up! Listen to me! We are going to the cabin!"

But his words fell on deaf ears. Casson lay utterly inanimate, his face as pale as chalk.

Bomba put his hand on the old man's heart. At first its motion seemed to have ceased, but after a moment the boy could detect a weak fluttering that showed life was not extinct.

Bomba chafed his companion's wrists and slapped his hands, but there was no glimmer of returning consciousness, and after efforts lasting a quarter of an hour or more without result the lad desisted.

There was nothing for it but to carry the aged naturalist back to the cabin. Over cleared ground this would not have been difficult. Casson was light and Bomba was strong beyond his years. But in the tangled jungle it proved no easy task, and the boy was panting heavily when he at last deposited his helpless burden on the floor of the hut.

Nearly half the cabin had been demolished, but part of the roof was intact and would furnish a partial protection against rain and sun. Bomba cleared away some of the foliage of the fallen tree until he had room enough to move about.

Luckily, one of the hammocks had not been damaged, and Bomba lifted the unconscious man into it. Then he set about brewing some of the medicines whose secrets he had learned from Candido, an old half-witted cabocle, who was accustomed to visit the cabin at intervals.

All through the night Bomba administered at regular periods a decoction of herbs to his patient, hoping almost against hope that it might prove effective.

But when the morning broke Casson was worse than the boy had ever known him to be before. He was burning with fever and he tossed about so violently in delirium that Bomba was afraid he would throw himself out of the hammock.

The lad made, therefore, a bed of branches on the floor, covered it with a blanket, and laid Casson on it. Then he got together a hasty breakfast and renewed his ministrations.

But all to no effect. Casson was plainly growing worse with every hour that passed. It seemed as though death were preparing to lay its hand on him.

Bomba was frantic with grief and anxiety. He was devotedly attached to the old man, who had always been good and kind to him. The thought of Casson dying and leaving him all alone was intolerable.

What must he do to avoid that calamity? What could he do?

He knew that some of the medicine men of the tribes, in addition to their supernatural pretensions, had a wide knowledge of medicinal herbs and were really gifted in their treatment of diseases. He thought of the Araos, a friendly tribe, that on more than one occasion had been of service to him. Hondura, their chieftain, would no doubt be willing to lend the help of Peto, a medicine man of great renown in that region.

But the Araos were too far away. Then, too, they might have shifted from their former location, owing to fear of the headhunters. He might search for days before he found them, and by that time Casson might be dead.

Then a wild thought came to him. How about Ruspak? To be sure, the man was his enemy. But he was skilful, and Bomba felt that he might be able to save Casson's life, either from fear of losing his own if he failed or as a result of bribes that might be offered him in case he succeeded.

That he would not come of his own accord was certain. Bomba would have to use strategy or force, perhaps both. But the boy felt that in either of these contingencies he would be more than a match for the wily medicine man.

It was a counsel of desperation, but Bomba had the conviction that only thus would he be able to save his companion's life.

He knew that Tocarora and his people could not be far away. Encumbered as they were by their wounded companions, they would have to travel slowly. He could easily catch up with them. Then he could watch his chance, and by hook or by crook get possession of Ruspak.

But how to leave Casson alone? Suppose the headhunters should double on their tracks and return. Or suppose an anaconda or a jaguar should come along and make the helpless man a victim.

Sorely perplexed, Bomba asked himself these questions, as he paced restlessly up and down before the cabin.

His problem was solved sooner than he had expected.

There was a crashing in the bushes and a great puma bounded into the clearing!

Bomba's first impulse was to reach for his weapons. But the next instant a look of pleasure came into his eyes as he recognized the newcomer.

He went up to the beast fearlessly and affectionately tweaked his ears and caressed the great shaggy head. The beast purred with pleasure and crouched like a dog at Bomba's feet.

"Good old Polulu!" murmured Bomba. "He has not forgotten his friend. Bomba is glad to see you."

The purring of the puma became more pronounced, and he licked Bomba's hand.

Their strange friendship dated back to a time when Bomba came across the beast, trapped by a falling tree which had broken his leg and held him captive. Bomba had released him, bound up his broken leg, and brought him food and water until the puma had fully recovered.

Polulu, as Bomba had named him, had ever since that time been the boy's devoted friend. More than once he had helped him in some dire extremity, the latest occasion having been when Nascanora had attacked the cabin. All his natural, ferocious instincts were subdued when in Bomba's presence.

"Listen, Polulu," said Bomba. "You came at a good time. Bomba wants you to stay and watch this cabin while he is away. Casson, too, is your friend. Casson is sick. Do not let any hurt come to the sick man."

He led the beast to the door of the hut and patted him till he sank down on his haunches.

"Stay here," said Bomba. "Do not go away until I come back. I will not be long."

His words and the gestures that accompanied them conveyed his meaning clearly to the puma, which settled down in front of the door like a great watch-dog as though for a long stay. Bomba knew that nothing could get inside that door as long as Polulu was alive.

Immensely relieved at the help that had come so opportunely, Bomba did all that he could to make Casson comfortable, gathered together his weapons, and saw that they were in the best of trim, and then, with a parting caress to Polulu, plunged into the jungle.

Before long he reached the place where Toca-rora and Ruspak had held their angry colloquy of the previous night. From there on, the trail of the headhunters was easy. They had made no attempt to disguise it, as they did not dream that the whites, even if alive, would have the audacity to follow it.

Still they had had a long start, and it was several hours before the freshness of the footprints warned Bomba that he was getting near them and would have to exercise more than his usual caution.

He had framed no special plan to effect Ruspak's capture. That would have to be dependent entirely on time and circumstance. It was manifestly impossible to take him from the midst of his comrades. The attempt would have meant quick and certain death to Bomba.

He must await his chance to find the medicine man alone. And when that chance came, if it should come, he must be prepared to grasp it instantly.

What he chiefly relied on was the habit of the medicine men of going into the forest alone in order to gather herbs and roots or to carry on their pretended interviews with the gods. On such occasions the tribesmen held aloof, thinking it to be sacrilegious to intrude on the meditations of their priests.

Such an occasion might present itself now, and if it did, Bomba would be ready to take instant advantage of it.

He knew now that he was close to the invaders. He caught their scent, and at times could hear ahead of him a crackling of the bushes as the members of the party pressed through them. It behooved him now to be extremely careful. His own life and that of Casson depended on his caution.

Soon his nostrils caught the sniff of smoke and he knew that the savages had paused and were lighting a fire for their midday meal.

He crept stealthily along through the underbrush until from a thicket so dense that he felt perfectly secure against detection he could see the encampment of his foes.

A meal was in process of preparation, and most of the men were busy about the fire.

Tocarora was seated at the foot of a great tree. His injured wrist was still giving him pain, as was evident by his restlessness and the twinges that from time to time convulsed his face. And that he was in a furious temper could be seen by his scowl and the snarling way in which he barked out his commands to his tribesmen.

Ruspak, the medicine man, was at the other end of the clearing, as far away from the chief as possible. It was clear that the breach between them had not been healed.

It was the first chance Bomba had had of study-ing the medicine man's face. It was one of great shrewdness and cunning. The priest wore a cir-clet of alligator's teeth about his neck, and his chest was tattooed with grotesque symbols, de-signed to impress the superstitious savages with his exalted position as their mediator with the gods.

Bomba was torn with anxiety and impatience as the members of the party ate, lingering long over the meal. But he felt repaid for his waiting when he noted that Ruspak, who had eaten little, was gathering from his pouch several curious objects such as were used by the native priests in their incantations.

"Where is Ruspak going?" growled Tocarora, as he watched the preparations surlily.

"I go into the forest to consult the gods," was the reply, as Ruspak rose to his feet.

"When will Ruspak be back?" questioned Tocarora.

Bomba waited in a fever of impatience for the medicine man's answer.

"That is for the gods to say," replied Ruspak impressively. "They take what time they will. Tocarora need not wait. I will follow and be with you before the sun has set."

The natives shrank aside as he stalked through them and was swallowed up by the jungle.

The path he took was at right angles to that the party had been following. Bomba wormed his way backward until it was safe to rise to his feet. Then he made a circuit that he knew would cut the trail that Ruspak was pursuing.

In a little while he could tell that he was nearing his quarry. He could hear the brush crackle as the man pushed through it. But he was in no hurry to spring his surprise. The farther Ruspak got away from his comrades the safer it would be to make the attempt that Bomba had in mind.

More than a mile had been covered before the medicine man found a location to his liking. He stopped in the shade of a great tree, made a little altar of stones and placed upon it small images of his gods.

Then he began his invocations, waving his hands in cabalistic signs, reciting what seemed to be a litany, and at times prostrating himself to the earth.

Bomba drew an arrow from his belt and fitted it to the string of his bow. Then, at a moment when Ruspak's back was toward him, Bomba stepped noiselessly into the clearing.

CHAPTER VII

HELD IN BONDAGE

BOMBA covered his human target with his weapon and spoke in a voice low but tense.

"Ruspak!"

The effect was electric.

The medicine man whirled about like a flash, surprise and alarm in his eyes as they fell on Bomba. Then he opened his mouth as though to shout for help.

"Do not call," warned Bomba, as he drew the arrow to its head. "If Ruspak calls, he dies!"

There was such menace in Bomba's eyes and death was so certain if the arrow left the bow at that short range that Ruspak obeyed.

"What do you want of me?" asked the medicine man in a strained voice. "How do you dare threaten with death a priest of the gods?" he continued haughtily.

"You shall not die if you do as I say," replied Bomba, not relaxing his grip on the bow. "I want you to come and help the white man to get well by your medicine."

"I thought he was killed by the tree that fell last night," muttered Ruspak.

"The tree did not hurt him," replied Bomba. "But he is very sick. You are wise in making sick men well. After you have made Casson well, you can go again to your tribe without hurt. I will give you presents."

Ruspak pondered for a moment, not that he had any way of escape from his dilemma, but because it did not comport with his dignity to yield too promptly to the demand of this boy.

"I will go," he said at last, beginning to gather up his small stone images. "But it will not be well if you do not see that no hurt comes to Ruspak."

"I do not speak with a forked tongue," replied Bomba. "You shall go in peace if you make Casson well. But we must go in haste, or Casson may be dead before we get to the hut. You must walk before me and do just as I say, for my hand will be on my knife and the knife is long and sharp."

They started off in the direction that Bomba indicated. From time to time Ruspak glanced behind him, always to find the boy watchfully regarding him and ready to punish him for any attempt to raise an alarm.

In a little while the white lad and the Indian reached the vicinity of the cabin. As they emerged

into the clearing a shriek of terror came from
Ruspak's lips. He had seen the puma stretched
before the door, from which the animal had not
budged during Bomba's absence.

The medicine man turned to flee, but Bomba
stopped him.

"He will not hurt you," he explained. "He is
my friend. But if I told him to, he would tear
you in pieces. Come here, Polulu."

The great beast rose and came toward Bomba,
who caressed his shaggy head, while Ruspak,
tightly held with the lad's other hand, looked as
though he were about to collapse with fright.

"You have done well, Polulu, and now you can
go to your hunting or to your cave," said Bomba.
"But come back again and stay near the cabin
so that you can come if Bomba calls. For Bomba
is in great trouble. Do not hurt this man as long
as he stays at the cabin. But if you see him
running off through the woods, he is yours."

Polulu seemed to understand perfectly, and
Ruspak trembled violently as the great yellowish-
green eyes rested on him for a moment. The
puma rubbed his head affectionately against the
boy and then bounded off into the woods.

What Bomba had said to him had been chiefly
for Ruspak's benefit, and that it was effective was
shown by a new submissiveness that had come into
the medicine man's attitude. It was clear, too,

that he had an added respect for Bomba. Anyone who had such a formidable ally as the great puma was not to be trifled with.

The boy and his prisoner went inside the hut, where Casson was still tossing in delirium.

"You see he is very sick," said Bomba. "But you are the greatest of the medicine men and you can make him well."

The flattery was not without its effect, and Ruspak was put at once on his mettle. His professional pride, as well as care for his own safety, was enlisted at once. He made a careful examination of Casson.

Under his direction Bomba brought some water from the stream. Then Ruspak took some herbs from the pouch he carried at his waist and, squatting on his haunches, began to prepare a brew, muttering incantations as he did so.

Having made his decoction, he began to administer it to Casson at regular intervals. After several hours had passed, the patient broke out into a profuse sweat, and soon after sank into a refreshing sleep.

Bomba was delighted at the evident improvement in Casson's condition, and Ruspak himself strutted about with his chest thrust out like that of a pouter pigeon. The hostility he felt toward the whites had abated considerably in the pride of his professional triumph.

"Ruspak is a great medicine man," said Bomba.

"Yes," admitted Ruspak complacently. "Ruspak is great. There is no greater among all the tribes. When he makes medicine the sick get well."

Bomba had prepared a good meal, of which they both ate heartily. A sort of truce had established itself between them, born of their absorption in a common task, that of making Casson well. For the moment the hatchet was buried, though each knew that before long it would be taken up.

After the meal was finished, they conversed for a time on indifferent subjects, with long intervals of silence. Bomba could see that Ruspak was far more intelligent that most of the natives with whom the boy had come in contact.

The thought came to him that probably Ruspak could tell him something of Jojasta, the medicine man of the Moving Mountain. There was nothing else that he desired so earnestly to learn.

For in one of his lucid intervals Casson had told Bomba that if he wanted to learn more of his parents he must get that knowledge from Jojasta. Casson himself had tried desperately but vainly to recall the facts, but his memory had failed just when the old man was on the point of disclosure. But Casson knew that Jojasta had the knowledge that he himself could not recall, and it had been agreed that at the earliest moment possible Bomba should make the journey to the Moving Mountain and try to get from Jojasta the facts that meant so much to the boy.

"Does Ruspak know Jojasta?" asked Bomba, breaking a long silence.

The effect of this innocent question on the medicine man was remarkable. He sprang to his feet and stood shaking as though with the palsy.

"Why do you ask?" he said. "Jojasta's name is not to be spoken lightly. He can strike like lightning from a distance when he wills."

"You know him, then?" persisted Bomba, astonished at the sensation his words had caused.

"Who can say they know him?" replied Ruspak. "I know that he is a great medicine man and that he dwells at the Moving Mountain with its Caves of Fire. He holds himself apart and knows many things. Men tremble before him."

"I do not need to tremble, for I do not wish to do him harm," replied Bomba. "I want only to ask him a question. Why should he hurt me for that?"

"Do you mean that you are going to seek out Jojasta and speak to him face to face?" asked Ruspak, as though he could not believe his ears.

"I will do so as soon as Casson is well enough

to be left alone," replied Bomba. "Jojasta is the man who may be able to tell me about my father and my mother."

"Does not Casson know?" asked Ruspak incredulously.

"He did know," answered Bomba. "But his mind has been bad since his head was hurt. He has tried to tell me, but he forgets. He thinks that Jojasta may remember, for his head is good and he does not forget."

Ruspak gazed at the boy sombrely as though he were looking at one doomed to death.

"It is foolish for one to put his head in the mouth of a jaguar," he said, shaking his head solemnly. "It is just as foolish for you to go to find Jojasta. He may smite you dead with one look from his eyes. He has always been ready to kill. And he has been worse than ever since the death of his white wife."

Bomba started.

"White wife!" he exclaimed. "Is Jojasta, too, white?"

"He is half white and half Indian," replied Ruspak. "But his wife was all white. She was lost in the Caves of Fire many years ago, just after her child was born."

"Child!" ejaculated Bomba. "She had a child? Was it a boy or a girl?"

"A boy," answered Ruspak. "He would have

Casson could have once more the full possession of his faculties!

Bomba tried again and again to draw out Ruspak on the subject, but met only with a stubborn silence. The medicine man evidently regretted that he had said as much as he had, and he kept looking around fearfully as though expecting every moment to be punished for his indiscretion.

He was not so reticent, however, when Bomba, baffled in his main object, asked him about the prisoners whom he had seen in the hands of the headhunters on the previous day.

"Yes," he replied, with a smile of hideous satisfaction that Bomba would have liked to strike off his face with a blow, "our people had good hunting. They came upon a camp of whites and took them all."

"Why?" asked Bomba. "Had they done your people any hurt?"

"No," replied Ruspak, with a touch of surprise in his tone, as though to ask what that had to do with it. "But the jungle belongs to those who are strongest in it. We were stronger than they, and so we took them."

"Have you killed them?" asked Bomba.

"Not yet," replied Ruspak. "They must suffer much before they die. It will be a great day for our men and our squaws when they hear the white people groan and scream. They will make them do this for a long time. Then they will cut off their heads and put them on their wigwams."

Bomba shuddered as he listened to the brutal program. His heart was wrung with pity for the captives doomed to such a fate—the same fate, he knew, that awaited him and Casson if they should fall into the hands of the invaders.

"Was one of the white people a woman?" he asked, after a pause.

"Yes," replied Raspuk, "a woman with hair as yellow as gold. It will be a wonderful head to put on the wigwam of Nascanora himself. There are many heads there now, but none like that."

He licked his lips in pleasure at the thought.

Bomba's blood boiled, but he refrained from comment. Too much indignation might arouse the medicine man's suspicions that he was intent on rescue. So it was with assumed carelessness that he put the question:

"They will not die, then, until you have taken them to Nascanora?"

"No," replied Ruspak. "Nascanora would be very angry if they were not brought to him alive, so that he could make a great festal day for all the tribe."

This knowledge brought comfort to Bomba. These white people were still alive and there was hope. He vowed to himself that he would do all

in his power to effect the release of the captives.

Such a task, he knew, would involve the risk of his own life. Why should he take that risk for people who were nothing to him?

He knew the answer as soon as the question occurred to him. It was because they were white. And he was white. It was the call of the blood.

It was very late now and he was tired. He stepped to the door and looked out.

On the edge of the clearing he saw a tawny form stretched out and heard a purring sound. Polulu was at his post.

"Polulu is here," he remarked casually to Raspuk, as he closed the door and slipped the bar into place. "I am tired. I will sleep."

And he knew from the look of terror that came into Raspuk's eyes that he could sleep in safety. Whatever treachery the medicine man had in his heart would not be put in practice while the great beast stood on guard.

The next morning Casson was better, and by night he had come again to consciousness, though still very weak. But it was plain that he was on the road to recovery.

For two days more he progressed rapidly, and then Ruspak recalled the promise Bomba had made him.

"I have made the white man well, and Ruspak would go to his tribe," he said.

Bomba was perfectly willing to grant this permission. Not for a moment had he been without uneasiness lest the medicine man's people should come back, searching for him. Now that the priest had done his work, Bomba was only too ready to have him go.

"It is well," he said. "I will tell Polulu, and he will not harm you. But Ruspak must swear that he will not tell his people where he has been nor that Casson and Bomba are alive."

"I will swear," declared Ruspak, though there was a furtive look in his eyes that belied his words. "But Bomba has said that he would give Ruspak presents."

"Bomba does not speak with a forked tongue," replied the lad. "What would Ruspak like to have?"

"A box of the sticks that spit fire," replied Ruspak, pointing to a box of matches almost apologetically, as though he feared he were asking too much.

"It is yours," declared Bomba, with a lordly air.

The medicine man grasped it eagerly, his eyes sparkling with delight. It was a new magic with which to astound his people. To him it was more than gold. And when Bomba also brought forth an old book with colored pictures, the priest's rapture was unmeasured. Here was wealth beyond the dreams of avarice.

Bomba opened the door and called Polulu to him.

"Do not hurt him," he said, pointing to Ruspak. "He has done well. Now he is going into the jungle. Do not go after him. It is the command of Bomba."

Polulu purred and rubbed his head against Bomba's hand, while Ruspak, none too well reassured, made a hasty exit into the jungle, with many a fearful look behind.

The word of the medicine man had not deeply impressed Bomba. At the moment when it was given it might have been more or less sincere. But Bomba knew that when Ruspak once more found himself with his fellows his old resentment would probably return, and he would reveal that Casson and Bomba were still alive. Then Tocarora and his band might return and this time meet with better success. The thought of Casson's head and his own adorning a headhunter's wigwam was not an alluring one.

He had not liked the look in the medicine man's eyes when he had given his promise.

He did not ponder long over the problem. With Bomba to think was to act.

He sent Polulu away with a caress and then returned to the cabin.

"Listen, Casson," he said. "Ruspak has gone. He has broken your fever, and you are getting well. He said he would not tell his people that we were here and alive, but I do not trust him. So I am going to take you away from here and put you where you will be safe."

The old man nodded listlessly. He was immersed in the apathy that Bomba knew so well. It mattered very little to Casson whether he lived or died.

Bomba moved about the cabin, getting their few belongings together. These he took to the boat that was hidden in the borders of the river that flowed at the back of the hut.

After he had stowed them away, he came back, lifted Casson in his arms and carried him to the little craft, where he laid him comfortably on a blanket.

This done, he took his seat in the canoe, and with a few thrusts of his paddle sent the boat into the center of the stream. There the current caught it, and as it was flowing in the direction Bomba wanted to go, he had little to do but keep his craft in its course.

It was necessary, however, for him to keep a sharp lookout and avoid passing under the trees on the shores, from any one of which an anaconda might dart upon them.

They had traveled for several hours and it was nearly noon when Bomba reached the goal of his journey.

An old cabin stood in a little clearing, extending back from the bank of the river. Bomba guided the boat to the bank and gave a call.

An aged woman came to the door, shading her eyes with her hand as she tried to make out her unexpected visitors. She was very old and her face was seamed with wrinkles.

"It is Bomba!" she exclaimed, and her face lighted up with pleasure.

"Yes, Pipina, it is Bomba," replied the lad, as he drew the boat up on the shelving edge of the bank. "He comes to you because he is in trouble and wants you to help him."

"Why should not Pipina help Bomba?" was the reply. "He has many times brought meat to Pipina when he has had good hunting."

"He will bring more," promised Bomba. "Listen, Pipina. Casson has been sick, but he is getting better. Bomba has to go away, and it may be one or two moons before he can get back. He does not dare leave Casson alone, because the headhunters are in the jungle and they want to kill him. So he has brought him to Pipina and asks her to take care of him. There is much food in the boat, and Bomba will hunt and get more before he goes on his journey. Will Pipina do this for Bomba?"

The old squaw assented heartily. She had been a widow for many years, without child.en or grandchildren, living alone and getting a meagre living from her little garden patch. Many times Bomba, passing that way on his return from hunting, had supplied her with meat, and she was deeply grateful to him.

She was skilled, too, in the making and administration of herb remedies, and Bomba knew that Casson could not be left in better hands.

A hammock was fastened up in the shelter, and Bomba put Casson in it. Then he transferred all his supplies to the hut. For the next two days he devoted himself to hunting, and to such good effect that he brought home much meat for Pipina to cure and stow away for the future.

During all this time he had clung to the hope that Casson might recover his memory sufficiently to make his journey unnecessary. Again and again he had questioned the old man about Bartow and Laura, but without result. Casson tried desperately to recall what he had once known, but failed. All he could do was to repeat that Jojasta would know.

So, then, there was no help for it! To Jojasta Bomba must go, if he would find out the mystery that surrounded his parentage. And this urge had become so insistent that the boy was willing to face all perils to arrive at the truth.

On the third morning after his arrival at the squaw's hut, after an affectionate farewell to Casson and repeated injunctions to Pipina, Bomba set out on his journey to the medicine man of the Moving Mountain.

From Casson himself and what he had been able to glean in his conversations with Ruspak, he had a fairly good idea of the direction in which he would have to travel, and he knew that he could get further information from occasional friendly natives as he went along.

He traveled by boat on the first leg of his journey, as the course he had marked out led past the cabin where he and Casson had lived for so many years.

An exclamation of surprise broke from his lips as he came in sight of the well remembered clearing.

The hut was gone! In its place was a mass of smoking ruins!

Ruspak then had broken his word. He had told Tocarora that the whites still lived. The headhunters had come back only to find themselves cheated of their prey. The water had left no trail. All they could do was to vent their vengeance on the cabin.

How Bomba blessed the premonition that had led him to take Casson to a place of safety!

The hut could be rebuilt, if not there, in some other location.

And the very fact that the headhunters had

been there had an element of satisfaction. For it showed that they had not got the start of him that he feared in the long journey to the Giant Cataract.

For all through the two days that he had been furnishing Pipina with supplies he had been haunted by the fear that he could not overtake them before they had got back to the main body of their tribe.

At any other time he would have welcomed their departure, and counted every mile a gain that intervened between them. But his heart was set on the rescue of the white prisoners, especially since the gruesome description by Ruspak of the fate that awaited them. It would have been bad enough had they all been men. But the thought of that woman with the golden hair in the hands of the torturers made Bomba grit his teeth with rage.

He hid his boat and set forth with all the speed consistent with caution that he could muster. He trusted his woodcraft and sense of direction to bring him before long in the vicinity of the marauders.

He had traveled for perhaps an hour when, on turning a curve where the trail bent sharply to the right, he saw in the path before him a great jaguar!

The beast's face was confronting him not more

than thirty feet away. It was evident that the creature was as much surprised as Bomba at the unexpected meeting.

But it had no thought of retreating. It saw before it a choice prey that it had had no trouble in finding or stalking and it had no mind to miss the opportunity.

It rose with a hideous growl and began to advance menacingly until it could get near enough for the deadly spring.

Like a flash Bomba fitted an arrow to his string, drew it to the head and——

The string broke!

The beast crouched for its spring.

CHAPTER IX

THE ANACONDA'S COILS

Bomba gave himself up for lost. There was no chance to retreat.

Then suddenly a great, long body launched itself like lightning from the bough of the tree directly above the jaguar. The next instant the beast was struggling in the coils of a giant anaconda.

The fight that ensued was terrific. The snake had enveloped the body, and its fangs had buried themselves in the jaguar's neck.

The jaguar twisted and writhed, tearing at the coils with its claws and teeth. Its instinct told it that if it could only wrench the reptile's tail from the branch, the latter would lose its point of support and its coils would be deprived of their crushing power.

But the snake held on stubbornly, and its coils tightened until Bomba could hear the jaguar's bones crack. That was the beginning of the end.

Gradually the beast's struggles grew fainter as the breath was pressed from its body, until finally a glaze stole over its eyes and the body grew limp.

The anaconda was taking no chances, and it kept up the inexorable pressure until the body of the animal was crushed into a shapeless mass. Then it began to unwind slowly in preparation for making a meal of its victim.

Bomba had watched fascinatedly as his two enemies, either of whom would have killed him without compunction, fought it out together. But he had no wish to face the anaconda, so now he beat a hasty retreat, not stopping until he was a long way from the scene of the battle.

He stopped only to put a new string on his bow and then resumed the journey that had come so near having a sudden and fatal termination.

He kept his mind centered on the jungle that he traversed, his eyes scanning every tree and darting from one side to the other to detect any lurking enemies. But this concentration did not prevent other thoughts coming into his mind from time to time.

Foremost among these were apprehensions for Casson. The old man had but a slender hold on life, and might at any time drift into the great beyond, even if he did not come to his death by violence. Bomba felt sure of Pipina. He knew that she would be faithful to her trust. But there was ever the haunting fear that Casson's hiding place might be discovered by his enemies.

Bomba wondered, too, about the fate of the four white prisoners, especially the woman with the golden hair.

Most of all he thought of the object of his mission, of Jojasta and the wonderful Moving Mountain. Would the Caves of Fire solve the mystery of Bartow, of Laura?

Impatient of the distance that separated him from the answers to these questions, Bomba moved forward more swiftly.

He was thirsty, and his jungle instinct told him that water was near. He swerved aside to the right.

He went forward eagerly, his thirst urging him on. But before he had gone many feet a sight met his eyes that caused him to stop suddenly, a scowl of anger darkening his face.

For about the pool were many snakes, some as thick as Bomba's arm, others as thin and sinuous as eels. The pool was well guarded. Safer to pass through a ring of hungry jaguars than to brave the deadly, writhing guardians of that water hole!

As silently as he had come, Bomba slipped backward through the jungle. He was wrathful and disappointed. His thirst seemed only the greater because he had been denied the means of gratifying it.

There would be other holes, but meanwhile

Bomba's thirst grew in proportion to his weariness. This part of the jungle was new to him. He must depend upon his instinct and to signs seen only by the jungle bred to lead him to water.

These did not fail him, and it was not long before he came out upon a shallow little brook flowing over the rocks and stones in its path with a pleasant, murmuring sound.

Bomba gave a cry of relief, flung himself face downward on the bank, and drank eagerly of the clear, cool water.

For a few moments he sat still and rested, and to beguile the time he took from his pouch the mouth organ that the white men, Ralph Gillies and Jake Dorn, had given him and played a crooning melody.

There was a slight rustling in the bushes near him and the wicked head of a snake appeared, upraised, its beady eyes fixed with a horrible intensity upon Bomba.

The boy's first impulse was to spring to his feet. But the snake was so near that Bomba knew it would strike before he could get out of reach.

So he did not move, but kept on playing, watching the snake out of the corner of his eye but otherwise betraying no knowledge of its presence.

Almost in the very act of striking the serpent hesitated, its malignant head for the moment rigid and motionless. The eyes became glazed as with a white film. Then the long body began to sway undulatingly from side to side, keeping time to the music.

Bomba was playing for his life, and he knew it.

He kept up the eerie strains without cessation until the snake appeared completely magnetized. Then inch by inch, still playing, Bomba moved backward until he had increased the distance between him and the reptile to fifteen feet.

Like a flash he leaped to his feet, turned and ran, nor did he slacken his speed until he knew he was perfectly safe.

Wonderingly, he caressed the harmonica, which for the second time had saved his life. What was there about the instrument that rendered his most terrible enemies helpless?

"It is magic—the magic of the white men," he muttered. "They know everything. And some day Bomba will know everything, for he is white."

For a long time the boy traveled swiftly. He reached, and passed, the place where he had first seen the four white prisoners from his observation post in the dolado tree.

There was no trace of their presence there, except the cold ashes of the Indians' campfire. The hapless captives were now no doubt on their way to the village of Nascanora. But his woodcraft enabled him to detect many signs that told him he was on their trail and not very far behind them.

Night was falling, and he stopped to rest. From the pouch at his belt he took a bit of roasted meat that he had prepared before he started. He had not brought much provision with him, as there was plenty of game in the jungle, and his bow and arrows could be relied on to procure him all he might need while on his journey.

He was munching contentedly on his bit of tapir meat when his quick ears warned him that all was not well in the immediate vicinity. He was conscious of vague murmurs, subtle rustlings in the forest about him, so slight that none but jungle ears could ever have detected them.

Bomba's senses were instantly alert. Danger lurked in the jungle all about him. Each tree or bush might conceal some shadowy, sinister form.

Luckily he had not yielded to the temptation to build a fire, which might have betrayed his whereabouts.

On hands and knees he crept stealthily forward avoiding entangling roots and vines by the sixth sense developed from long residence in the jungle.

As he went forward silently, he became more and more certain that the woods were full of gliding figures like his own. At any moment he might meet one of these sinister shadows.

Once a sharp spiked thorn touched his shrinking flesh, and Bomba thought it the edge of an Indian's knife.

If he had leaped to his feet then to grapple with his imagined foe, that gesture might well have been one of the last that Bomba would ever have made, due to the clue it would have given to his whereabouts in that grim game of hide and seek.

But he realized in time what it was that had torn at his flesh. For a moment he was as motionless as the trees about him. Then with redoubled caution he slithered, snakelike, through the heavy underbrush.

There came a sudden ghostly rush on both sides of him, like the rustling of swamp grass beneath a gentle breeze. The shadows were taking substance!

Bomba dropped upon his stomach and waited, the strong brown fingers of one hand clasped upon his faithful knife.

Suddenly there rose from the depths of the jungle a dreadful sound, a shrill, agonized scream of terror!

CHAPTER X

THE FIGHT IN THE DARK

THAT cry tore at Bomba's heart like a physical pain.

He sprang to his feet, all sense of personal danger gone. He ran with the swiftness of a deer toward the spot from which the shriek had come.

The jungle was no longer silent. There were sounds of a struggle, the short grunts of Indians and the hoarse, panting cries of white men.

Then came the scream again, shrill and terrible.

Bomba set his teeth and tore aside some bushes that screened the struggle from his eyes.

Down in a hollow two savages were scuffling with a third shadowy figure. Bomba's eyes, used to the darkness, saw that this was one of the white captives—the woman with the golden hair.

Even as he looked, Bomba saw the savages bind their victim and throw her to the ground.

Bomba's eyes flashed and his fingers tightened about the hilt of his knife. In a moment he saw what he could do.

The branch of a tree swung low over the hollow. Like a cat, Bomba climbed the trunk. Like a snake he writhed his way out along the branch until he hung directly over the three figures.

With the swift sureness of a jaguar he sprang upon the back of one of the Indians and sunk his knife deeply. Before the second savage could recover from his bewilderment Bomba was upon him, and he went the way of the first.

Swiftly Bomba turned to the captive.

She had uttered one startled cry as Bomba had sprung from the tree. Now she raised herself to a sitting posture. Her eyes were wild and terrified. When Bomba approached her, she shrank back in fright.

The boy bent over her, caught her hands in his and slashed at the cords that bound them.

"Quick!" he cried. "We must go."

As she still shrank from him, Bomba seized her hands again and half-dragged her to her feet.

"Come!" he cried. "I am your friend. I will help you. Come quick!"

Avoiding the twisting and moaning bodies on the ground, Bomba led his shuddering companion into the shelter of the heavy underbrush.

Their escape from the Indians was only a confused memory to Bomba after that night. A dozen times, shadowy, sinister figures passed so close to them that it seemed only necessary to reach the length of his arm to touch them.

Bomba's companion allowed herself to be led, unresisting, where he willed. She seemed in a half-dazed state from terror and exhaustion.

At last she stumbled and fell and could not get up again. Bomba knew that they could go no farther.

"Where am I? Who are you? What is going to happen to us?"

The words were only a whisper, but Bomba put his hand quickly over the woman's mouth. She shrank from him, and the gesture had a curious effect upon the jungle boy. He felt shy and awkward.

No wonder she shrank from him. He must have seemed alien to her, hardly different from the savages from whom he had rescued her. She knew he was formidable. She had seen him strike with lightning strokes. He was of the jungle, and everything in that fearsome place held terror for her.

They sat crouched in the underbrush for a long time, neither moving nor speaking. Bomba's every sense was alert to note the slightest movement, catch the faintest sound. But when time passed and deep silence still prevailed, the boy began to hope that they had really escaped their enemies.

If the Indians had given up the pursuit for the night, they would probably resume it in the morning. But before dawn Bomba planned to be far from that spot with his companion, the strange white woman with the golden hair.

While Bomba was revolving these thoughts in his mind, he was startled by a slight touch on his arm. He reached quickly for his knife before he realized that it was his companion who had touched him. Bomba had never felt a touch so soft and light.

"Are we safe? Do you think they have gone?" came from her lips in a whisper.

"Yes," replied Bomba, wondering why it was so hard for him to speak at all. "I think they have gone for to-night. But they will be back. Before the sun comes up in the sky we must go. Now you must sleep."

"Go where?" murmured his companion, taking no notice of his last words. "Where can we go?"

"Away from this place to another where I shall take you," said Bomba, and marveled at the smothered gasp that came to him from the darkness. Had he said anything queer? he wondered.

He waited for a moment, and when his companion did not speak, said again:

"Now you must sleep."

"Sleep!" cried the woman, with a passionate intensity that amazed and troubled Bomba.

"How can I sleep? How can I ever sleep again?"

Bomba said nothing, because he could think of nothing to say. And when his companion began to sob softly, her face buried in her hands, Bomba sat rigid and miserable.

She dropped off to sleep at last, falling fathoms deep into the slumber of sheer exhaustion.

Though Bomba was weary, too, he did not once close his eyes during that long vigil. Responsibility sat heavily upon him. This was a woman, a white woman, and he, Bomba, stood alone between her and the countless dangers of the jungle.

Her touch was soft like the flutter of a bird's wing, and her hair was golden, the color of the sun.

But she had shrunk from him, and Bomba's heart was suddenly heavy. Perhaps she thought that he was a caboclo or an Indian. His skin was dark enough.

But he would tell her when she awoke that he was white. Perhaps she would not shrink from him then.

Through the night Bomba sat with his bow and arrows ready and his knife across his knees. Sometimes there were rustlings in the bushes, and once a pair of yellow eyes gleamed out at him from behind a tangle of vines.

Bomba fitted an arrow to his bow. There was a swishing sound, a snarl of pain. The eyes disappeared and there was a crashing through the underbrush. The sound dwindled into the distance, and Bomba smiled to himself.

"Bomba shoots well even at night," he said, half aloud. "Not even the jaguar comes too close."

After awhile the deep shadows of the jungle began to lift. One by one surrounding objects became clear to Bomba—the castanha trees bending their nut-laden branches close to the earth, the tough, lacy vines trailing almost at his feet.

Bomba shifted restlessly and turned so that he might see his companion. To his surprise and embarrassment, he found that the eyes of the golden-haired woman were wide open and staring at him.

Now she lifted herself stiffly to a sitting posture and shook the disheveled, beautiful hair back from her face. She glanced at Bomba's bow and arrows and knife ready to hand, then back at the boy's face.

"You have been sitting here all night?" she asked, in a low, sweet voice. "You have been keeping awake all night guarding me?"

Bomba smiled, white teeth flashing in his dark face.

"Once there was a jaguar," he said. "It did not stay long."

The woman shuddered as though she were cold

and drew her hunting jacket closer about her. Then she regarded Bomba with an intent, curious look.

"It was very brave for you to do what you did last night," she said.

Bomba thought that he had never heard sweeter music.

"I thought that you were one of those men at first," the woman went on, with a shudder. "Now I can see that you are not like them."

Bomba's breath came quickly. His eyes shone with hope. She would know! He would not have to tell her!

"Why," she exclaimed in amazement, "you are a white boy!"

"Yes," cried Bomba exultantly. "I am white! Bomba is white!"

CHAPTER XI

ELUDING THE HEADHUNTERS

THE woman caught hold of Bomba's arm. Her face was white and strained, and there were dark circles under her eyes.

"Then you will help me?" she cried in an agony of entreaty. "You will help me find my husband and my brother and my son? They are all gone —captured by the Indians again. At this very moment perhaps they are being tortured. Oh, I can't bear it! I can't bear it!"

She sprang to her feet, a wild light in her eyes. Bomba drew her gently back to the ground again.

"We must not talk loud," he warned. "There may be Indians all around us. I will try to help your people, but we cannot go too fast. Tell me about them first. Were they with you last night?"

With a tremendous effort the woman gathered herself together. She bent close to Bomba and spoke quickly, now and then glancing uneasily about her at the jungle shadows.

"The Indians raided our camp one night and captured us all," she said. "It was horrible!"

Her voice had risen, and she paused, seeking for self-control.

"I saw you afterward," said Bomba. "I saw you tied to trees in the jungle."

The woman gave a sharp cry.

"Please!" she begged. "I can't bear even to think of it! One night my brother succeeded in loosening his bonds. He cut us loose and we escaped. But we were lost. We tried to find our way back to our camp, but could not. The hardships we suffered——"

She paused, and Bomba read tragedy in her eyes. Again he felt tongue-tied and embarrassed. He longed to say something to comfort and reassure her, but did not know how.

"Then last night they found us again," she went on, again sending a terrified glance into the jungle shadows. "When they rushed out upon us and surrounded us, I became almost mad with terror. I broke away from the others, but two savages followed me. They had just caught me when you came."

She looked at the boy searchingly, curiosity regarding him once more breaking through her grief and terror.

"You were splendid!" she said. "How could you possibly get the better of those two frightful savages—and you only a boy? You must be very strong as well as very brave."

Bomba glowed beneath this praise. But he had little time to enjoy this strange warmth about his heart, for almost immediately his companion reverted to her own terrible problem.

"All I know is that my husband and my brother and my poor boy are again in the hands of the Indians." She shuddered, and then added, stretching out her hands toward Bomba:

"Oh, isn't there anything we can do, any way we can find and save them?"

"We will try," promised Bomba, stirred deeply by the desperate appeal. "First, eat some of this."

He drew out from his pouch the remainder of the strip of meat he had been eating and that he had put away when alarmed by the Indians.

This food he offered to his companion, and was puzzled when she drew away and declined to touch it.

"I am not hungry," she explained, trying to cover up her shudder of disgust. "I could not eat just now."

Puzzled and vaguely distressed, Bomba sank his own white teeth into the tapir meat.

"You must eat," he said, regarding her with a troubled frown. "I will find you eggs of the jaboty or fish from the stream. You cannot go hungry."

"I will eat later," she promised, to appease him. "Yes, you shall find me some jaboty eggs."

Bomba flung the last bit of tapir meat into the bushes, and with a lithe movement rose to his feet.

"We will go now, and look for your people," he said.

His companion got to her feet, but was so weak that she stumbled and had to cling to a bush for support.

Bomba frowned.

"You are hungry," he said. "You were wrong not to eat the meat when Bomba gave it to you. It would give you strength."

"No," the woman protested, "I am just stiff and sore from lying on the ground. I am not used to it, you see."

"Yes, a hammock is better."

"Or a bed."

"A bed?"

"Yes. Don't you know? But come, we must be on our way."

She started forward, but after a step or two swayed a little and again put out her hand to steady herself.

Bomba came over to her quickly.

"Maybe you will lean on Bomba," he said shyly, with a flash of his white teeth. "I am strong."

The woman regarded the sturdy brown figure of the lad, looking in his puma skin like some youthful god of the old mythology, and a look of admiration, blended with profound gratitude, came into her beautiful eyes.

"You are a fine boy!" she exclaimed. "You are about the size and age of Frank. My poor, poor Frank! Shall I ever see you again?" and her voice broke into a sob.

"We will find him," said Bomba reassuringly. "Soon the sun will be red in the sky. We must go while the shadows are thick in the jungle."

They slipped off into the heavy underbrush, two silent shadows themselves. For a time, Mrs. Parkhurst—for that, she told Bomba, was her name—leaned heavily upon Bomba. The privations and hardships of her terrible adventure had borne hardly upon her. She was no longer the strong, active woman she had been when she had lightheartedly accompanied her husband into the jungle. What had then promised to be full of romance had now turned into a drama replete with horror.

However, she had great native courage, and anxiety for her family gave her strength and drove her on to effort that under a less strenuous urge would have been impossible for her after all she had already gone through.

Gradually the stiffness left her limbs and she

walked more easily. Bomba was almost sorry when she took her hand from his shoulder and walked on unaided.

For some time they were forced to proceed with the utmost caution. It was Bomba's idea to return to the spot where he had first come to the aid of Mrs. Parkhurst in her frantic struggle with the Indians.

Not far from there, she had said, her husband, brother and son had been captured. He would examine this spot and see if he could gather clues that would aid him in following the trail the savages had taken with their prisoners.

He had no idea what he should do if he came upon the headhunters. His quick wit would tell him that. He would find them first, then act.

They came upon no Indians nor signs of them, and Bomba began to hope that they had given up their pursuit of the woman with the golden hair, content with their recapture of the other members of the party.

If this were so, part of Bomba's problem would be solved. Instead of busying himself with eluding pursuit, he himself could become the pursuer and be able to take the initiative into his own capable hands.

Mrs. Parkhurst marveled at Bomba's knowledge of the jungle. Naturally, she could remember no details of the path they had traveled in their mad flight of the night before. It was all a distorted, hideous nightmare to her; a stumbling through impenetrable, terror-filled darkness; a horrid memory of cruel hands reaching out to pull her back into misery and captivity.

So now when Bomba went surely and steadily on toward the scene of the struggle, hard, sinewy muscles rippling beneath his dark skin, quick eyes darting to right and left to search out the slightest movement in the jungle, her curiosity regarding the boy returned a hundredfold.

She longed to question him, but when she made the attempt Bomba motioned her to silence.

"Better not speak yet," he warned her. "Better wait till we are sure the Indians have gone."

At length they reached the scene of the struggle.

The bodies of the two savages were gone. At the sight of the spot it seemed as though the woman's strength would give way. She shrank back, put her hands over her eyes and cried brokenly:

"John! Frank! Where are you? Oh, what are they doing to you?"

"Come!" said Bomba urgently. "I think we will find them. Come with me."

For Bomba had picked up the trail of the Indians. To any eyes not jungle trained, the signs of recent passing would have been too faint to notice. But to the lad they spoke with clearness, and he did not once hesitate or falter.

Mrs. Parkhurst followed close behind him. Though she said nothing, she knew that her strength was fast deserting her. It would be impossible for her to continue much longer in that rough going without resting.

Then she heard a grunt from Bomba, saw him pause and fit an arrow to his bow.

CHAPTER XII

THE GROWL OF THE WATERS

THE woman gave a start as she noted Bomba's gesture.

Indians! They must have overtaken them at last.

But almost as the arrow left the bow, Bomba gave a cry of triumph and darted out into a clearing. His companion followed cautiously, and saw him bending over a tapir. The arrow had pierced the animal's heart, and it had died instantly.

Bomba dragged it into the shelter of the bushes.

"Now you will have something fresh to eat!" exclaimed the boy, his dark face agleam with pleasure. "We are lucky. The meat of the tapir is good."

"But the Indians!" cried his companion, forgetting for the moment her hunger and fatigue. "We must follow them. We must not waste a moment."

"We do not waste time when we eat," said

Bomba, already busy stripping off enough of the skin for him to cut a steak. "Besides, we must think now, and we can think while we eat."

"Why do we have to think now more than before?" asked Mrs. Parkhurst.

Bomba pointed silently through the trees.

Following the gesture, the woman saw through the dense underbrush a gleam of water.

"The river," said Bomba. "The Indians have crossed it in canoes."

At first Mrs. Parkhurst could not understand —or would not.

"We cannot follow them," explained Bomba patiently. "If we had a boat we could. But there is no boat."

The woman took an unsteady step backward, and put her hand for support against the trunk of a tree.

"Then we cannot follow them," she said in a dazed way. Her face, which had been white before, was so ghastly white now that Bomba was frightened.

"We will try to go around," he told her quickly. "We will go down the river and find a way to cross. Sometimes there are logs that make a bridge. Or we will make a raft."

"But surely you can swim!" she exclaimed. "I am a good swimmer. Let us go over that way."

"There may be alligators," said Bomba gravely.

"And there are sure to be piranhas. They would eat the flesh from your bones. But some way, we will get across. Now," as he bent above the tapir, "we shall have food."

The woman turned away with a shudder as Bomba expertly removed the skin and cut out a chunk of the meat. She was feeling faint and weak, and the sight of the blood that stained Bomba's hand filled her with repulsion.

Bomba sensed this feeling, and again was vaguely troubled. He was white, and yet was not like the other white people. He did not shudder at the sight of blood.

His work was quickly done. While the woman sat aside, her face buried in her hands, Bomba built a small fire and, using a long stick for a spit, began to roast the meat.

As the odor assailed her nostrils, Mrs. Parkhurst took her hands from her face and crept closer to Bomba. She had been for a long time without food, and for the moment her hunger made her forget everything else.

When Bomba held out the stick to her with the roasted meat at the end of it, she took it eagerly and ate it with a relish that she would not have thought possible.

Bomba watched her with approval. He found another stick and began to roast a big piece for himself.

A curious thought struck him. Whenever he had seen the natives roasting meat, the men ate first and gave the women what was left. Why had he not done the same? Was it perhaps because he was white? He was glad that he had done it.

As she ate, Mrs. Parkhurst felt herself strengthened and refreshed.

Watching Bomba, intent upon his task, she was prompted to say to him:

"You know so much about the jungle—as much as though you were an Indian."

"More, much more," said Bomba, not with any special pride, but as a statement of fact. "They do not know the jungle as I do. They do not speak the language of the animals or have their friendship. They do not know the name of each leaf and flower and make friends of the trees."

"And you do all these things?" asked Mrs. Parkhurst gently.

Bomba glanced quickly at her, then again at the fire.

"I have many friends in the jungle," he said simply.

"But you are a white boy." Mrs. Parkhurst was puzzled and curious. "How is it that you live in the jungle? Surely your are not all alone."

"I live with Casson," replied Bomba, as though that should tell her everything.

"But your father and mother?" The woman was gently insistent. "Is this Casson your father?"

A dark shadow crept over Bomba's expressive face. Mrs. Parkhurst saw it, and was sorry that she had asked the question. What right had she to intrude upon the boy's privacy? But it was now too late to take it back.

"Casson is my friend," said Bomba slowly. "He is very old, and his mind is not good. He cannot remember about my father. I do not know who he is."

"And your mother?" asked the woman softly. She was greatly interested in this strange jungle boy, and the thought came to her that she might be able to do something for him, if she ever again should reach shelter and safety.

At this question about his mother, something welled up in Bomba that made him feel that he must tell this gentle, golden-haired white woman all he knew. Some instinct told him that she would understand and sympathize with him.

"I am trying to find out about my mother—and my father too," he said.

The meat, well done, dangled at the end of the long stick. But for the moment Bomba had forgotten it.

He told her about Ruspak, and what the medi-

cine man had said about Jojasta. He told her,
too, how Casson had spoken the names Bartow
and Laura, and had urged him to go to the
Moving Mountain to see Jojasta and find out
from him who these people were and what rela-
tion they bore to Bomba.

"If the girl that Ruspak said was lost in the
Caves of Fire was Laura, perhaps she was my
mother," said Bomba, staring moodily into the
fire. "And if she is, then Jojasta, the medicine
man, must be my father."

Mrs. Parkhurst nodded gravely. She had finished the tapir meat and now threw the stick away
from her.

"That may be so," she agreed. "Though you
are very different from him in nature. I have
heard my brother speak of this Jojasta, and he
says he is cruel and a tyrant."

"I hope he is not my father," replied Bomba.
"He is only half-white and I would be the same.
I want to be all white like you.'

The heart of the white woman reached out
toward the lonely lad.

But when she would have said something to
comfort him Bomba jumped to his feet and looked
with troubled eyes out toward the river. It was
rising, and far off in the jungle could be heard
a low, ominous murmur.

There was rain somewhere, many miles away

perhaps, but torrential rain. Bomba knew what rain meant to the rivers of the jungle. There would be an overflow into the forest. There might even be a pocoroca, the dreadful tidal wave of the Amazonian delta.

Even as Bomba looked and listened there came a swift rush of rain through the trees. The ominous murmuring in the jungle increased.

Mrs. Parkhurst was standing beside him. She, too, was alarmed.

"What is that noise?" she asked. "It sounds like the roaring of a wild beast."

"It is the river rising," said Bomba. "There have been great rains somewhere and it will soon be higher than the banks. Come, we must get to higher ground."

But Mrs. Parkhurst caught him by the arm.

"Our camp was by the banks of some river," she said. "Perhaps if we keep near the banks we will find it again. I do not want to go too far from the river."

Bomba nodded thoughtfully.

"We will keep near the river, but not near enough to be in the way of the pocoroca if it comes." he replied.

"The pocoroca!" exclaimed his companion. "You mean the great tidal wave? No, we must not be in the way of that!"

"Come," said Bomba, and once more led the

way through the jungle, keeping some forty or
fifty feet from the bank of the river.

The parrots screamed overhead and the
monkeys howled as they fled to shelter. The sky
opened and let down the rain in what seemed to
be a solid sheet. The wind swept through the
forest, bending trees beneath its fury, hurling
castanha nuts like gigantic hailstones to the sod-
den ground.

The sullen roaring of the river increased. The
turbulent surface of the waters showed black
and menacing in the peculiar grayish-green light.

Mrs. Parkhurst followed Bomba with dogged
courage. Her yellow hair was loose, and enveloped her in a golden mist. Her clothes were torn,
her hands scratched and bleeding. Her breath
came in gasps as she strove to make headway
against the furious wind.

Bomba tried to urge her to still greater speed.
They were still on low ground. If they could
reach a higher point, they might avoid the menace
of the growling stream.

But even with his help, the woman could only
stagger on, her strength almost exhausted.

Bomba's darting gaze rested on the surface of
the river. The swelling waters had suddenly re-
ceded, showing parts of the river banks that a
moment before had been covered with water.

Bomba knew what that meant. The tidal

wave! The beast was crouching for its spring!

There was a breathless pause, an unearthly stillness. Even the shrieking of the frightened parrots was stilled. The hot breath of the tropics blew softly on the faces of Bomba and his companion as they stood rooted to the spot in awful suspense.

Then, with a roar like that of a thousand jaguars, the tide of the river turned and the relentless force of unchained waters overflowed the river banks, bearing trees and jungle growths before its terrific onslaught.

"Quick!" shouted Bomba, though his voice was lost in the thunder of the torrent. "Run for the trees!"

CHAPTER XIII

IN THE GRIP OF THE TORRENT

NEVER in Bomba's life had he been so thankful for his strong arms, his iron muscles, as in that moment when not only his own life but that of the white woman as well depended upon them.

He half-led half-carried her into the jungle, away from the swelling rush of the river. He had but brief time to act. He stopped before a stout tree that seemed to be strong enough to resist the power of the waters.

To climb it was their only hope of escape, and that but a slender one.

He picked up his companion as though she were but a featherweight and held her so high that she could clutch a low-lying branch.

"Hold on!" he shouted.

Like a flash he darted around to the other side of the tree, and went up its trunk like a monkey. His feet firmly established on the branch, he reached down, drew up his companion, and placed her in the fork of the tree.

She helped as much as she could, driven to

almost superhuman effort by the danger that threatened.

Nearer and nearer came that terrible roar. The tidal wave was upon them!

They saw it coming through the trees, a solid mass of water, fifteen feet high, dashing toward them with the irresistible force of a cataract.

They could note the way it uprooted jungle growths, snapping the trunks of trees as though they were saplings. Mrs. Parkhurst cried out in terror, though her voice could not be heard above the tumult.

Trees were going down like tenpins all around them. The branches, as they swept by, bit at them, tore them with their sharp twigs and spines.

Then with a horrible roar the torrent was upon them. Bomba gripped the branch of the tree with all his strength, one arm wound tightly about his terrified companion.

Down went the tree with a sickening, swooping descent, the roots torn from the ground by the tremendous force of the current. In a moment they were submerged by the merciless wave.

An eternity of bursting lungs, while the cruel fingers of the torrent sought to tear them from their support! Logs and débris hurtled past them, battering them, bruising them, threatening to crush the life out of them, as they clung des-

perately to the branch that could be their only
salvation.

Then slowly, groaningly, the tree swung clear
of the main current and grounded on a little
knoll, where the branch lifted its half-drowned
burden a little above the turbulent surface.

As the air rushed into their tortured lungs,
Bomba felt the form within the circle of his arm
grow limp.

Shaking the water from his hair and eyes, he
looked at his companion. She had fainted.

He was sore and bruised in his every muscle.
His whole body ached. But he summoned up all
his strength to retain his grip with one hand on
the branch and with the other arm to sustain his
helpless burden.

It brought some comfort to him to see how
rapidly the waters sank after the passage of the
tidal wave. It would not be long before he could
drop from the tree and fight his way with his
companion through the flooded portion of the
jungle to high and dry ground.

In the distance he could hear the passing of the
pocoroca. Muttering like some ferocious giant
balked of his prey, it grew fainter, dying at last
into grumbling—into silence.

Rain still fell in gusts, making more dismal
the scene of ruin in the wake of the tidal wave.
Débris of all sorts floated about the foot of the

tree. Tarantulas, scorpions and spiders in great numbers floated on the surface of the waters, washed from their positions on shrubs and bushes near the river.

Bomba waited until he thought that it was safe to descend. Then slowly, cautiously, he slid down the trunk of the tree, bearing with him the unconscious woman.

To his relief he found that the water had fallen until it reached only to his waist.

As he turned to avoid a log that was floating past, he felt the burden on his arm grow lighter. Mrs. Parkhurst had come back to consciousness.

She struggled to regain her feet, while the dazed expression in her eyes gave way to one of terror.

"Where are we?" she cried. "Oh, I re- member!" She shuddered and put a hand before her eyes. "That horrible wave! We were be- neath it drowning, drowning—oh, it was hor- rible!"

"But we are safe now," Bomba assured her. "The pocoroca has passed and now we can go on our way again."

"And you have saved my life once more," said the woman, looking gratefully at Bomba. "What a brave boy you are! I owe you everything."

Bomba had no words to answer this. For while praise from this white woman warmed his heart and made him strangely happy, he had no way of telling what he felt. In spite of the curious kinship he felt with all white people, he was still tongue-tied and shy before them.

But perhaps Mrs. Parkhurst read the secret of his thoughts in the glowing dark eyes he turned upon her. At any rate, she patted his hand as though it had been that of her own lost son, and thereafter leaned upon him and followed him with perfect confidence.

They were forced to proceed slowly, not only because of the difficult going caused by the flood but by the weakness of Mrs. Parkhurst. The reaction from the submersion was upon her, and her limbs trembled beneath her. Horrors sufficient for a lifetime had been compressed into her experiences of the last few days, and had strained her almost beyond endurance.

After a long struggle through the débris-clogged, flooded jungle, they came out finally on higher ground. Here traveling was easier, though they were still forced to proceed slowly and cautiously.

After a half hour of this journeying, Mrs. Parkhurst stumbled and almost fell. But she recovered herself, clung to Bomba's arm, and staggered on.

"It's of no use," she gasped at last. "I can't go a step further!"

Bomba had been sniffing the air.

"Wait here," he said, as he helped her gently to the ground.

Quick as a panther, he left her side and started to climb the trunk of a near-by tree. The woman stared after him, wondering, half frightened.

In a few moments the boy dropped to her side again. His dark eyes glowed as he pointed through the trees.

CHAPTER XIV

THE JUNGLE CAMP

"There is smoke down there," stated Bomba.

His tone was so exultant that Mrs. Parkhurst's weary eyes lighted with a sudden hope.

"A camp?" she exclaimed.

Bomba nodded.

"White man's camp. Some natives and a white man around a fire. Your camp, maybe."

The woman swayed dizzily and Bomba put an arm around her for fear that she would faint again.

But she pushed his arm away.

"Oh, take me there quickly, Bomba, quickly!" she cried. "If there is a white man there, it may be my husband—it may be my brother! Bomba"—her voice became only a faint gasp, her eyes pleaded wildly with the lad—"you did not see a boy down there, a boy like you, about your size?"

Bomba shook his head, gently releasing her fingers from about his arm.

"I did not see one. But he may be there."

He had no time for further speech, for Mrs. Parkhurst had already sprung away from him and was running through the jungle.

Bomba reached her in a few long strides and caught her by the arm.

"Not that way," he said. "Down there."

Though Mrs. Parkhurst allowed him to show her the way she moved forward as though on wings. In her excitement and exaltation she had found renewed strength. Hope of what she might find and fear of what she might not find quickened her steps.

They soon saw the flickering of the campfire among the trees. About the fire and a little removed from it, some natives were seated in a semi-circle, chewing dried beef and farina.

Closer to the fire, his back toward Bomba and his companion, sat a white man, his shoulders hunched in a way that betokened melancholy, looking into the flames.

A twig cracked under the woman's feet.

Instantly the natives were standing. The white man sprang up and leveled a rifle in the direction of the sound.

"Gerry!" cried the woman in a shrill, strange voice. "Put down that gun. It is I—Rose!"

With a hoarse cry the man dropped his weapon, and as Mrs. Parkhurst stumbled into the clearing caught her in his arms.

"Rose!" he cried brokenly. "I have searched all over for you. I thought——"

"Yes, Gerry, I know," cried the woman, as she returned her brother's embrace. "But, Gerry, where is John? Where is my boy?"

She stepped back and looked at him with frantic eyes. Bomba stood uneasily in the background, uncertain whether to stay or go away.

"I don't know, Rose," Gerard Hicks put both hands on his sister's shoulders and looked at her steadily and sorrowfully. "I managed to get away in the darkness. I succeeded in getting back to the camp and bringing some of our helpers together. Since then we have been searching constantly for you and for John and for the boy. But cheer up, my dear. We will find them yet."

Mrs. Parkhurst sank down with a little moan upon the ground and stretched out her shivering hands to the warmth of the fire.

"It is like a terrible fantastic dream!" she cried. "Why, oh, why, did we ever come to this horrible place? And now John is gone! And Frank— my poor, poor boy!"

As Mr. Hicks bent over his sister to comfort her, Bomba, feeling strangely out of place in this intimate scene, turned to steal away into the jungle.

One of the natives saw him and, suspicious of his intentions, put his hand on his shoulder.

Bomba shook off the hand angrily with a muttered exclamation.

Mrs. Parkhurst turned at the sound, and before Bomba could again slip away called to him to come to her.

Bomba came reluctantly, still wrathful at the native and shy before the curious eyes of the white man.

"Who is this boy?" asked the man, as he took in the lad from head to feet.

"He is a white boy, Gerry, who has lived all his life in the jungle. He saved me from the Indians, and it is owing to him that I am here with you now, safe and alive."

The haggard eyes of the white man lighted up with instant welcome. He caught Bomba's brown hand in a firm and hearty grasp, eloquent of gratitude.

"Thank you, my boy," he said. "If you have served my sister you have served me too. Come now and have some food with us, while you, Rose, tell me what has happened since the savages fell on us back there in the jungle."

Bomba came forward slowly and squatted near the fire. He looked neither to the right nor left of him, but kept his eyes fixed steadily on the flames.

He was still shy, but memory of the strong grip of the white man's fingers upon his own filled him with a great warmth. It was puzzling, that pressure of hand upon hand. The natives never exchanged handshakes. Only the white men did. Bomba half understood that it meant friendship, trust.

The natives, seeing that Bomba was on friendly terms with the golden-haired white woman and her brother, abandoned their attitude of hostility and served him with food with the same civility they showed to their masters.

Bomba took the food gladly and ate ravenously, while Mrs. Parkhurst recounted to her brother the story of their adventures in the jungle.

While she was speaking, Bomba felt that Mr. Hicks was regarding him curiously. When she again repeated his name, the white man slapped his knee with his hand and gave vent to a short laugh.

"I imagine this is the same lad I've heard Gillis and Dorn talk about," he said.

Bomba turned to him eagerly.

"Do you know Gillis and Dorn?" he asked.

"I surely do," replied Mr. Hicks. "We're in the same rubber company. They told me about a boy named Bomba, a white boy who had lived in the jungle all his life and dressed like a native. And they told me all about the way you saved their camp and their lives the night they were attacked by a horde of jaguars. Well, my boy, it's great luck for us that we, too, happened to run across you!"

Bomba felt that there was an added bond between them after that, and he was happy to know that Gillis and Dorn remembered him. How often he had thought of them and how he had hoped that he might see them again!

When he had finished his dinner of beef and farina—food not nearly so pleasant to his jungle-trained palate as jaboty eggs and tapir meat—Bomba became restless. He was eager to be on his way once more. A great deal of time had been lost already, and there was in him a great impatience to reach the Moving Mountain, to meet Jojasta and get from the medicine man the truth concerning himself.

"I hope you find your boy," he said, as he got to his feet, a fine, sturdy figure in the light of the fire.

"But you will look for him, Bomba?" pleaded the bereaved mother, taking the boy's hand in hers. "You will try to find him and bring him back to me? Say you will. Promise. Promise."

Bomba looked down at the tear-stained face of the white woman with the golden hair and made a great resolve.

"I will look for him," he promised. "If I find him, I will bring him back to you."

Then the white woman rose to her feet and

put her arms about Bomba and kissed him as
though he had been her own son.

It was the first time anyone had ever kissed
him, and the maternal tenderness expressed by it
thrilled him to the heart.

"Then good-bye, Bomba," she said, trying to
smile through her tears. "I will look for you,
pray for you to come back to me safely and bring
Frank with you."

She fell back, and as Bomba turned and stumbled blindly into the jungle he could hear the
sound of her sobbing.

A feeling, half sadness, half exquisite joy,
flooded Bomba with an intensity that almost made
him afraid.

"That must be what my mother is like," he
thought, and repeated the words aloud, "My
mother."

With a sudden passion, his hands upflung
toward the crests of the palm trees waving above
his head, he cried:

"I will know! I will know! Jojasta, who is
my mother?"

CHAPTER XV

THE MOUNTAIN WAKES

BOMBA's mind was engrossed with several problems as he journeyed through the jungle, his face set resolutely toward the Moving Mountain.

First among these was the promise he had made to Mrs. Parkhurst to lead her husband and son back to her, if their paths should cross his during his journeyings toward Jojasta and toward the explanation of the secret that remained behind the closed door of Casson's mind.

He would do this if possible. If a single clue came to him that would lead to the discovery of the missing ones, he would follow the trail wheresoever it led.

But he could not spend time wandering about aimlessly on the mere chance of coming across them. It was urgent that he should reach Jojasta as soon as possible, for he must leave Casson no longer than was absolutely necessary. Duty toward his old friend came before his newly acquired allegiance to the woman with the golden hair.

He traveled rapidly for several days and nights. He had no trouble in finding plenty of game in the jungle and about the water holes. This he brought down with his bow and arrows. In the streams there were many fish, and when he tired of these as a diet he sought and found the succulent eggs of the jaboty or forest turtle.

He lived well and traveled swiftly, and though at night yellow-eyed beasts of the jungle sometimes prowled just without the circle of his campfire, they seldom ventured within range of his deadly aim.

He looked constantly for signs of the missing white man and boy, but never once in those days and nights did he pick up a trail that led to them.

This depressed him, and he thought often of the white woman and her brother at their lonely campfire. His only comfort was the hope that by this time the missing members of that circle might have returned to it.

Often he tried to imagine what the white boy who was Frank would be like. He had met white men now and a white woman with hair like the sun. What would a white boy be like—a boy of about his own age? Would he be as strong and tall as himself?

The thought awakened in him vague longings for the companionship that had always been denied him. He knew that he wanted to see this white boy who had a mother—a soft-voiced white mother with hair like the sun.

But as the days wore on and Bomba drew nearer to the region of the Moving Mountain with its Caves of Fires, every other thought grew subordinate to the one great object of his journey. His pulses were fevered with growing excitement.

He had heard many wonderful things from Ruspak about this fearsome place, so clothed with mystery. In a day now, perhaps less, he would reach it and be able to see for himself.

As Bomba progressed it seemed to him that the jungle growth was becoming more dense, the parrots gaudier in color, the air hotter and more breathless.

That night he cooked his dinner of wild hog meat and turtle eggs with the conviction that on the following morning he would for the first time gaze upon the Moving Mountain.

All that day of travel there had been strange swayings in the ground beneath his feet, earth trembles that had filled the jungle lad with uneasiness. Always before even the muddy bottom of the ygapo had had a certain firmness under his tread. Bomba did not understand an earth that shivered as though with jungle fever. And because he did not understand, he was filled with vague alarms.

Often during the late afternoon Bomba had

taken to the trees, like his friends the monkeys, and made rapid progress swinging from branch to branch. Once he saw the wicked head of a boa constrictor and dropped to the ground, only to feel the earth trembling worse than before.

All day it had been like that. But to-morrow— he would know!

Through the long watches of that night Bomba did not close his eyes. He felt hot and parched, as though he himself were the victim of jungle fever. But in his heart he knew that never in his life had his body been stronger, his brain more keen and alert.

What was that strange fire, then, that blazed within him, filling him with a wild restlessness so that it was intolerable to lie through the long hours of darkness waiting for the shadows to lift so that he might start on the last lap of his journey?

Dawn came at last, gray shadows streaking through the jungle.

Bomba piled wet leaves on his fire, stamped upon them and reduced the embers to a smoking smudge.

Then on, with a lifting of the spirit and that strange, wild fire tingling through him, lending wings to his feet.

On and on he went, while the shadows lifted before the advancing dawn. But Bomba missed the dewy freshness of the early morning that lay upon that part of the jungle where he and Casson had had their hut. Here it was dry and hot long before the morning sun had blistered the jungle growth to a dry and crackling brittleness.

There was a breathless hush hanging over everything. The ground still trembled and shook as on the day before. Only the shrieking of monkeys and gaudy parrots and the occasional clear fluting of a bird broke the deep silence.

He was in a hilly section, and for a long time he climbed steadily, taking the ascents almost as swiftly and easily as though he had been on level ground.

Suddenly he paused.

From somewhere just ahead of him there came a curious grumbling sound unlike anything he had heard before.

Quick as a cat, the lad climbed to the top of a great dolado tree. It rose high above its fellows, and from its crest Bomba could see for a great distance on all sides of him.

As the lad looked, his grip on the tree tightened and a smothered cry was torn from his throat. There before him, its huge bulk rising majestically far above the valley, loomed the dark forbidding face of the Moving Mountain!

And it was moving!

As Bomba stared, his whole being filled with

terror, the side of the mountain, outlined blackly against the rosy glow of the sky moved.

Slowly it moved on in its ponderous, mysterious way, while Bomba watched and his heart grew cold. Strangely he felt, as though that terrible mountain were moving toward him to bear him down beneath its weight and crush him, as he had seen a great stone crush the head of a reptile.

Then, while he watched, unable to stir, scarcely able to breathe, there came a horrible, rending noise. Before Bomba's staring eyes a section of the towering mountain came loose and slid into the valley beneath! The earth itself had split wide open!

CHAPTER XVI

A FRIGHTFUL EXPERIENCE

Simultaneously with the fall of the mountainside a crimson tongue of flame darted from the crest of the Moving Mountain and the dolado tree swayed from side to side in a mad fantastic dance of nature.

Bomba strove wildly to cling to his hold. But he felt his fingers torn loose as though by some gigantic hand, lost his grip, and went hurtling downward through space.

He clutched at the waving, ghostlike branches as he fell. He would have his hand on one, his eager fingers almost closed around it, when it would be whisked away, leaving him grasping at the empty air.

Scratched, buffeted, terrified, Bomba continued the hurtling descent through swaying foliage and branches. The roar of a giant cataract was in his ears and above it rose a terrible hissing sound as though from all the serpents in the jungle.

It seemed to Bomba as though the earth rose up to meet him. He fell in a clump of thorn-filled bushes and a sharp tingling ran through him, as though his body had been penetrated by the poisoned arrows of Indians.

Half-dazed, he tried to extricate himself from his painful bed. It was hard to do so, for the earth was rocking madly, and each time he tried to struggle to his feet away from the torturing bushes he was flung backward again, to be impaled upon the needle-pointed darts that sank deep into his flesh.

Lashed by fear and half-crazed by pain, Bomba finally tore himself free and tried to stand upon his feet, his body a quivering mass of agony.

But he could not stand. The rocking earth beneath his feet flung him from side to side as though he had been a spineless thing devoid of all strength. He was beaten and bruised. The hissing noise increased in volume until it seemed to fill the jungle.

And still new terror was in store for him. For suddenly the trees and bushes about him seemed full of life. Wild jungle creatures fled past him, some so close that by reaching out a hand he could have touched them.

At first he thought that they had come to attack him, and, feeling his helplessness, he turned and tried to flee. But he could only blunder blindly on, shaken to his knees again and again by the writhings of the earth beneath.

Still the jungle beasts came in hordes, small terrified animals that scurried between his legs and tripped him up, pumas and jaguars that crowded him so closely that at times he could feel their hot breath upon him.

There were snakes, too, some as slender as whiplashes, here and there a great boa constrictor or anaconda from which he shrank in horror.

One immense old jaguar, maddened with fear, plunged straight into Bomba, knocking him down, treading on his prostrate body, and continuing his wild flight into the jungle and away from the Moving Mountain.

Trembling, exhausted, Bomba dragged himself to his knees, wondering that he was still alive. But as he gazed at the hordes of flying, maddened beasts and reptiles, the truth came to Bomba.

They did not think of harming him, they paid no more attention to him than they did to the trees and bushes that stood in their line of flight, they had forgotten for the moment all their natural enmities. Like himself, they were terrified by this mad freak of nature and were only intent on fleeing from the wrath of the Moving Mountain.

On, on, staggered Bomba, the earth moving in billows beneath his feet. He was bleeding from the wounds inflicted by the thorn-filled bushes.

His strength was almost at an end. Before him the earth cracked and opened, disclosing a yawning hole.

Bomba, thrown to the earth again, found his fingers clutching at the edge of the hole. He drew them back only in time. For the edges of the wound in the earth closed again with a horrible, grinding sound.

Shuddering, Bomba rose to his feet and staggered on. At any moment the ground might open again and let him down into such a hole, closing again before he could scramble out.

Then all was still. The hissing noise ceased. The trembling of the earth stopped. The trees, which a moment before had been weaving and swaying in their fantastic dance, stood motionless. Not a breath of air stirred the foliage. The change was as quick as though caused by the wave of a magician's wand.

Bomba drew a long breath of relief and drew himself up on his trembling limbs and leaned weakly against a tree.

How could he know that this was merely a lull in the storm, one of those breathless pauses during which Nature gathers herself together for a still more vicious and deadly onslaught?

He could not know, but, leaning there, his breath coming in sobbing gasps, strength beginning to flow back into his bruised and beaten body, he dared to hope that the wrath of the Moving Mountain had been appeased, and that the nightmare dance of natural forces had come to an end.

It was only a moment before he found out his mistake. Another convulsion of the earth, more fierce than any which had preceded it, threw him to the ground. Again there came that sinister hissing, that terrible roar. The red flame, spurting from the crest of the Moving Mountain, rose high in the air, suffusing the skies with a weird, unearthly glow.

Bomba shouted aloud in irrepressible terror. The mountain towering above him seemed as though it were bent on crushing him. He plunged madly away in the opposite direction.

A tree, uprooted, flung itself across his path. Bomba sprang backward, and at that moment felt the touch of a fiery dart upon his hand.

He lifted it and saw upon its back a drop of water. He raised his face and felt upon it the sting of another tiny dart.

Boiling water! Down from the skies it was coming upon him in scalding, blistering drops that promised soon to become a flood!

CHAPTER XVII

THE JAGUAR'S DEN

WITH a hoarse cry, Bomba turned and staggered on, his hands outstretched, groping for some place of shelter.

Where to go? How escape that boiling flood which menaced him with death in one of its most horrible forms?

The drops were coming faster now. Bomba struggled blindly on, one hand upraised to protect his eyes.

He struck suddenly against some thing hard with such force that the impact threw him backward on the ground.

Struggling to his knees, Bomba found that the obstacle was a huge rock in which, by some freak of nature, an opening had been hollowed out that seemed just large enough to admit his body.

Desperate with the pain of the blistering drops that had already burned his flesh in a dozen places, Bomba flung himself flat upon his face and began to push himself into the opening feet first.

It was slow work, for the opening was so narrow that he had to turn and twist in order to force his body into it. Meanwhile the scalding water of the geyser continued to fall upon his head and shoulders, causing him intolerable pain.

But it was done at last. Bomba found himself wholly beneath the shelter of the rock. But he was wedged in so tightly that he could scarcely breathe, and the pressure of the rough rock against his burned flesh was almost unbearable. He wondered how long he would be able to endure that torture.

Outside of his shelter still sounded that sinister hissing, blending with the roar of uprooted and falling trees. The earth was still quivering beneath him, and the rock above him cracked and groaned and threatened to fall apart.

With the feeling of an animal in a trap, Bomba wondered what would happen if the earth should open here, as he had seen it do in the jungle. He would be caught beyond the possibility of escape. He would fall into the yawning hole, and when it closed again with a snap like a wild beast's jaws, he would be within those jaws.

The hot water was coming down now in such volume that the spray from it was flung into the narrow tunnel in which Bomba lay. To escape it, he edged his way still further back, and suddenly realized that one foot had more leeway than formerly. He felt it slip backward into a wider place.

This made him pause in the clutch of a new fear. What was that wider space behind the narrow tunnel? Almost certainly a cave. And if a cave, some beast of the jungle might be lurking there.

In front and behind he was threatened by terrible possibilities.

To work his way outward again to the open jungle and expose himself to torture and death beneath a flood of scalding water was unthinkable.

But he could not remain long where he was. His cramped position was agonizing. His body was on fire. He felt as though he were incased in a bed of redhot coals.

But to go backward into a cave whose occupant was unknown, to be torn to pieces perhaps by cruel maw and claw!

Then he remembered the hordes of wild jungle creatures fleeing in terror before the wrath of the Moving Mountain. Perhaps, after all, the cave might be empty.

He decided to take the chance. He could not stay where he was. He could not go forward. So he would go back and trust to fate.

Slowly, painfully, repressing the groans that his pain tried to wrench from him, Bomba worked his way backward inch by inch, not knowing but that at any moment he might hear a snarl or feel a vicious jaw clamped on his leg.

He worked his legs through without much difficulty, but when it came to his broad shoulders it was a different matter. He wedged himself in so tightly that at one time he thought he would be able neither to go back nor come forward again. He would die there of hunger, if nothing worse. And no one would ever know—not Casson, nor the white woman with hair like the sun.

But at last with one tremendous effort, a heave of his shoulders that seemed to tear the flesh from them and extorted a cry of agony from his lips, Bomba wrenched himself free and fell backward into the darkness of the cave.

For a few moments he lay there, gasping for breath and gritting his teeth against the pain that flooded him.

Then one arm, groping cautiously, came in contact with a soft, furry ball. His fingers sprang back as though they had touched flame. At the same moment a growl echoed through the stillness of the cave, followed by another and another.

Bomba gave a hoarse cry and fumbled for his knife. But the next moment he laughed aloud in a relief so great that it was almost pain.

His eyes, now accustomed to the darkness, made out that the authors of these brave growls of defiance were baby jaguars, helpless kittens, who thought it proper in the absence of their elders to make some show of hostility toward this uninvited stranger in their home.

Bomba put out his hand and they growled again, spitting at him this time by way of added defiance.

The boy laughed and drew one of the kittens toward him, fondling and mauling it gently, and delighting in its show of baby ferocity.

But this mood of playfulness did not stay with him long. Nor did his relief in finding the mother jaguar absent from her lair persist.

She had left the cave, perhaps, to investigate the strange trembling of the earth. She might even have been seized with panic and fled with the others. But she would not go far nor stay away long. She would not leave her young to starve.

The narrowness of the entrance to the cave was Bomba's one hope. She would have to squeeze her way through and come slowly. He would have her at a disadvantage, and his arrows or his revolver would do the rest.

But could she come in some other way? Was the tunnel beneath the rock the only entrance to the cave?

Roused to action by this apprehension, Bomba got to his feet and made the round of the cave, the baby jaguars sniffing and snarling at his heels.

His groping hands found no other opening. He was satisfied at last that the only entrance to the cave was that by which he had entered.

So he sat down near the hole to wait, his bow and arrows close beside him, his knife and revolver at hand.

It was a test of courage more severe than those which afford room for action. To sit for hour after hour, not daring to relax vigilance for a second, dropping with fatigue, anguished with pain, yet doomed to remain constantly alert, listening for the slightest sound within the tunnel, expecting to see at any moment a pair of yellow eyes glaring into the darkness, was a task that demanded nerve and valiance of the highest type.

Once or twice Bomba nodded, only to straighten up again instantly.

An hour dragged on and nothing happened.

The ground was still trembling beneath Bomba as he sat cross-legged on the floor of the cave. Outside he could hear a steady, muffled roaring, as of a mighty wind.

He wondered if the heavens still rained those fiery drops. More than once he was tempted to make his way into the open again to find out. But at the very moment that he would be wedged in the opening the jaguar might enter the cave and find him helpless. Better to wait until the beast appeared, and by killing her find his way clear to the jungle.

Bomba might have the mate to reckon with, too. That he knew well—although the instinct of

the male to return to its young was not so great.
But even if he did appear, Bomba would have
only one to deal with at a time. There would
simply be two dead jaguars instead of one.

He had plenty of time to think, and his thoughts
were anything but pleasant ones.

What was the meaning of this terrible wrath
of the Moving Mountains? Why had it chosen
the moment of his appearance for such an out-
break? Was it angry because he, Bomba, had
come to wrest a secret from the heart of it?
Were the tremblings of the earth and the rain of
fiery liquid warnings to him to desist from a pre-
sumptuous quest and return to Casson while there
was yet time?

As the time passed doubt and perplexity
weighed still more heavily on Bomba. Should he
go back to Casson without seeing Jojasta and con-
fess failure? No! A thousand times no! Better
to brave the wrath of the Moving Mountain,
better that the earth should open and swallow him
forever than that he should go back without knowing the secret of his parentage, without learning
what was meant by Bartow and Laura, that secret
that was locked behind the closed door of Casson's
mind.

What was that?

From the mouth of the cave came a low snarl,
hair-raising in its menace. Bomba's heart beat

rapidly as through the darkness he saw two yellow points of light.

Bomba sprang back and lifted his bow. The great beast had entered so stealthily that its body was already squeezing itself through the narrow wedge not four feet away. Bomba could feel its hot breath upon his face.

He drew the arrow to the head and let it go. The beast gave a wild scream and fell back. Bomba fitted another arrow to his string to make assurance doubly sure.

There was a terrific explosion, a roar as though the earth itself were disintegrating.

Bomba felt the ground rock beneath his feet, then rise as though it would lift him to the sky. Above him was a grinding, rending sound, and the roof of the cave split open.

Bomba felt himself flung to a distance. He fell on his back. A terrible weight bore down upon his chest.

Then a black curtain descended and all was dark.

CHAPTER XVIII

THE CRY FOR HELP

How long Bomba lay unconscious he had no way of knowing. The sun was high in the heavens when he once more opened his eyes and stared vaguely about him.

His chest hurt dully. It was hard for him to breathe. Dirt and stone were piled upon him in profusion.

He lifted a hand weakly and brushed some of the débris off him. The weight on his chest was lightened sufficiently for him to raise himself on one elbow, slowly and painfully, and look about him.

A scene of desolation met his eyes. On every side were fallen trees, piled-up rocks, masses of earth, and dead animals.

He wondered why he himself was not dead. He remembered again the jaguar and the fight in the cavern. Then had come the noise, the rending and tearing, the letting in of light, the destruction of the cave in which he had been trapped.

Why had the Moving Mountain, which had

wrought so much destruction to other living
things, spared his life? Had its wrath been appeased? Had its demonstration of power been
intended simply to humble him and put him in
the proper frame of mind to approach the dreaded
medicine man who seemed to be the dominant
spirit of the place?

The Mountain was still now, the rain of liquid
fire was at an end, the earth once more unmoving
beneath Bomba's body. A strange stillness
brooded over the district, a stillness like that of
death.

Bomba drew himself painfully to his feet and
established to his joy that none of his bones were
broken. He could move about, although his whole
body was bruised and sore.

It was then that he saw what had saved him
from a terrible death.

Above his prostrate body two giant rocks had
fallen and had wedged against each other in such
a way as to form a tent over him. This had de-
flected stones and dirt from their course, and they
had plunged on down the mountainside instead of
descending with crushing force on Bomba's prostrate form. It seemed to the boy as though a
miracle had been performed in his behalf.

Having moved about until he had got his blood
in circulation and recovered the use of his limbs,
Bomba took stock of his situation.

He was sore and shaken, his body a mass of cuts and bruises. But the fact that he was still alive and that the jungle was still again—once more like the place he had always known—made his injuries seem light to Bomba. He was in such splendid physical condition that his wounds always healed quickly. He would find some water and bathe and cover himself with river mud, his sovereign remedy for bruises, and to-morrow he would be well.

But he must have food, and he looked about him. There were dead animals all about him. Most of them were small and had been killed by the fiery rain before they had had time to flee from the vicinity.

Bomba selected one of these and prepared the meat. Then he gathered some small sticks and made a fire. The meat was quickly roasted, and Bomba ate voraciously.

The meal at an end, he felt immensely strengthened. Once more he was aflame with eagerness to reach the Moving Mountain and question the formidable Jojasta.

He would go now, while everything was quiet and the spirit of the Mountain was placated.

As he journeyed on again, as swiftly as his bruised and aching legs would permit, he was consumed with curiosity to see again the huge, majestic bulk of the Moving Mountain, of which he had had little more than a glimpse before the earthquake and toppling mountainside had made him think only of preserving his life.

It had lost for him now something of its terror. To his untrained mind, the saving of his life had been a good omen, a sign that the ultimate wrath of the Spirit of the Mountain would not again be vented on him.

His progress was slow, because of the fallen trees across his path. But his eagerness to find Jojasta kept him doggedly at his task.

Presently he came to the place from which he had first beheld the Mountain. Again he climbed a tree and saw the dark, majestic height of it outlined against the clear blue of the sky.

The Mountain was quiet to-day, and that gave Bomba confidence. Only over the top of it was there the slightest movement, and this was furnished by a pale gray cloud that floated low over it, shifting and changing shape with the breeze.

That cloud did not worry Bomba as it would if he had known more about the nature of volcanic mountains. He slid lightly to the ground. His heart was glad, and once more excitement and hope rioted within him.

Downward he went, ever downward, into the valley until he reached the foot of the Moving Mountain. Looking up at it from the base, Bomba was again filled with awe and fear.

The great mass of rock and earth rose menacingly above him. To climb its steep sides one had to be as sure-footed as a mountain goat.

There were great bare spaces along its face, as though the foliage and verdure had been eaten away by some plant disease, and yawning caverns pockmarked the surface.

Somewhere upon that mountain dwelt Jojasta, who held the secret of Bartow and Laura.

Bomba hesitated but for a moment, and then plunged boldly into the undergrowth at the base of the mountain, working his way slowly upward, clinging to the tough vines and pulling himself up by them, as he felt for toeholds on the mountain's side.

Higher up, the going was not so difficult. The trees and bushes did not grow so closely together, and there were greater stretches of the bare, arid ground that Bomba had marked from below.

As he rounded the rough face of a great projecting boulder, Bomba came upon one of the yawning holes that studded the cliff.

Curious, he ventured forward and took a few steps within the cave. Suddenly a hot blast struck him in the face with the force of a blow.

As he stumbled backward, gasping, a tongue of fire shot from the back of the cave and enveloped him in a flaming red mist.

Coughing, choking, Bomba fell on his face,

while the flame crackled above his head for a moment and then drew back.

"The Caves of Fire!" cried Bomba, feeling that the wrath of the Moving Mountain had again descended upon him.

He did not dare to stand, for fear of being shrouded in a second burst of flame.

So he wormed his way backward on his stomach, holding his breath so as not to inhale the heated, noxious gases with which the place was filled.

Just as he reached the cool, blessed air outside, there came to Bomba a sound that chilled his blood and almost made his heart stop beating.

It was a cry for help, the cry of a human being in agony and terror. It came from the Caves of Fire!

CHAPTER XIX

A DARING RESCUE

THE cry that startled Bomba was so poignant, so despairing that it thrilled him to the marrow.

He could not ignore that appeal, could not think only of his own safety with that agonized cry ringing in his ears.

Swiftly he returned to the cave. There was no flame now. But to Bomba the black hole was a sinister thing, for somewhere within it lurked an enemy more ferocious than any beast of the jungle.

Again came that wild, wailing cry.

Knowing that he might never come out again, Bomba plunged into the cave. The air within was hot and stifling. Fumes of sulphur choked him. It was as black as the blackest night. He could see nothing, could only grope his way forward with hands outstretched, stumbling, falling, getting up again. Each moment he expected to see the hungry flame again dart forth and envelop him in that blistering, red mist.

"Where are you?" he cried hoarsely. "Who is here?"

A voice answered so close to him that Bomba was startled.

"Here! Here! Oh, help me!"

Bomba groped toward the sound. His hand touched something—something rough and bushy. It was hair, the hair of a human head.

"Get up," commanded Bomba. "The fire will come again. We must get out while there is time."

"I can't get up," came the voice, and now there was hope mingled with the fear in it. "My foot's caught. It's wedged between two stones."

His reason told Bomba that he had only a moment to act. He felt swiftly along the body until his hand reached the feet. He felt of the imprisoned foot, and as he tried to pull it loose a sharp cry broke from the lips of the hapless prisoner—a cry instantly suppressed, as though it had been wrenched from him against his will.

"I must move the stone!" Bomba muttered to himself.

The air was getting hotter, more stifling. A weird, red glow began to suffuse the cave. Bomba knew that the red terror would strike again.

His great strength served him well. Putting all the force of his strong, young shoulders into the effort, he strained to move the rock that imprisoned the foot of the victim. It yielded grudgingly, inch by inch, until a cry came from the prisoner:

"It's loose! My foot is loose!"

At the cry, Bomba turned from the stone and, stooping, wound his muscular, young arms about the body of the captive. It seemed to him to be the body of a boy.

The weird, rosy glow in the cave deepened to a lurid red. With a hissing noise, a lambent tongue of flame darted from the depths toward the mouth of the cavern.

With an arm about his companion, eyes shut against the searing flame, Bomba staggered toward the entrance to the cave.

Exhausted, choking, Bomba summoned his last reserve of strength and pushed his companion out on the steep slope of the mountain, out of the reach of the flame.

He himself followed, slipping and sliding, not caring if he rolled to the foot of the mountain. Nothing mattered at the moment, except to escape from the breath of the fire demon.

A narrow, outflung ledge of rock stopped his descent abruptly. He rested there for a moment, gasping, as the air rushed back into his tortured lungs. Then he drew himself to a sitting position and looked about for his companion.

Bomba's eyes narrowed, and a strange look came into them—a look at once eager and shy.

Not ten feet from where he had brought up was a lad of about his own size—a white boy with a shock of closely cropped yellow hair.

Bomba had seen white men and a white woman. Now before him was a white boy, a boy who came from that mysterious world outside the jungle of which Bomba knew almost nothing.

The heart of the jungle boy filled with a great longing to speak to this being of another world. He wanted to tell him that he, too, was white, though all his life he had lived in the jungle. But he could not speak. Shyness held him, and he could only gaze at the lad with the yellow hair and the blue eyes the color of the sky.

The white boy had been beating at his clothes, where tiny fingers of flame ran through them. He wore a gray, tattered shirt, so ragged and torn that it was hard to say how it managed to cling to his shoulders. His trousers were gray and had once been tucked snugly into the tops of high jungle boots. Now they were as ragged as the shirt and hung loosely from the belt at his waist.

Having beaten out the last treacherous spark, the yellow-haired boy looked up and saw Bomba's brown eyes fixed upon him.

He stared, started to speak, thought better of it, and contented himself with taking in the strange appearance of the boy with the puma skin wrapped about him.

"I say," he said at last, when the silence was
becoming uncomfortable, "are you the one that
dragged me out of that sizzling hole up there?"

He was frankly curious, and this curiosity
served to increase Bomba's shyness.

"Are you?" the white boy persisted.

"Yes," said Bomba, and stopped.

"That was bully of you, and I can't thank you
enough, for you sure saved my life. And, say,
I'll tell the world that you've got some strength!"

Curiosity gave way to admiration as the eyes
of the young fellow went to Bomba's strong
brown shoulders.

"You moved that rock as though it had been a
pebble," the white boy went on. "Gee, what
would I give to have a pair of arms like yours!
And it was mighty plucky of you to risk your own
life for mine. I guess if you hadn't come along
just then, I'd be nothing but a cinder by this time.
I say," he added, with a glance upward toward
the cave, the mouth of which was once more bleak
and gray, "what kind of a place is that, anyway?"

"It is one of the Caves of Fire," said Bomba
gravely. "There are more of them in the Moving
Mountain."

"Then I should say that the Moving Mountain
was a jolly good place to keep away from," was
the reply.

Bomba was puzzled.

"The Moving Mountain is not jolly," he said.

The white boy laughed, and after a moment of bewilderment, Bomba's own white teeth flashed in a smile. After that, the strangeness fell away from them, and they spoke like old friends.

"What's your name?" asked the yellow-haired boy, after a moment. "I'd like to know who it is I have to thank for saving my life at the risk of his own."

"They call me Bomba," said the jungle lad.

"Bomba what?" came the query.

"Only Bomba. I have no other name."

"I never heard the name before, but it's a nice one and seems to fit you. I'm Frank Parkhurst."

"Frank!" exclaimed Bomba exultantly. "I have been looking for you. You are the son of the white woman with the soft voice and the golden hair?"

"My mother!" There was suddenly an agony of entreaty in the other boy's voice. "Have you seen her? What do you know of her? Is she safe?"

Bomba nodded.

"I left her in the camp of the white man," he said.

Frank leaped to his feet.

"Then my father and my uncle—do you know that they got away safely?" he cried.

"Your uncle was at the camp, but your father had not come back," replied Bomba. "Your mother told me to look for him and for you. I have found you, but I do not know where your father is."

A shadow dimmed Frank's eager face.

"We escaped together," he explained, turning to Bomba and speaking quickly. "Another tribe of Indians attacked those who were holding us prisoners, and in the confusion we got away. But it was at night, and in trying to avoid the Indians I missed my father. I have been looking for him ever since and trying to find my way back to the camp."

"How did you get in the Cave of Fire?" asked Bomba.

"I was caught on the mountain yesterday, in the earthquake," replied Frank. "When the geyser began to spout boiling water I crawled inside the cave for shelter. But before you came the place began to grow hot and glow with that queer, red color, and I tried to get out. But I fell over those rocks and got my foot caught, and there I was like a rat in a trap. It wasn't any fun, I can tell you, especially when the fire began to run back and forth in the cave. Believe me, I thought I was a goner until I heard your voice and you came to my help. But say," he added eagerly, "are you sure that you know the way back to our camp?"

"Yes," answered Bomba. "I will take you there. But first I must see Jojasta."

Frank looked disappointed and puzzled.

"Who is Jojasta?" he asked.

Bomba explained as quickly as he could, which was not very quickly, seeing that the other lad was immediately and keenly interested and interrupted him to ask questions at almost every sentence.

"So Jojasta lives here on this mountain," mused Frank Parkhurst when Bomba had finished. "And when you have found him he will tell you all about your father and mother. I don't wonder that you want to find him so badly. I would, too, if I were in your place. But I wish it were all over," he added. "I've had all I want of the Moving Mountain, and I'm crazy to get back to the camp and find out about my father."

"It will not take long, I think," said Bomba. "You can stay here, if you like. Then I will come back after I have seen Jojasta, and take you to your people."

"No, no!" cried Frank, dismayed at the thought of being left alone in that place where he had suffered such torture of mind and body. "Let me go with you."

"Then we will go now." Bomba leaped to his feet and glanced at his companion. "Can you walk fast?" he asked.

"I'll say so," replied the boy sturdily. "There's

a lot of fight left in me yet. Lead on to old Jojasta."

The ways and words of the white boy were strange to Bomba, but he liked them. And there was a wiry strength in the slender city lad that was astonishing. Bomba set him a hard pace up the rugged side of the mountain, and though Frank panted with the exertion and was forced to stop now and then to rest, he kept on with a dogged courage that won the admiration of the hardier jungle boy.

As they climbed higher and higher, they became aware of the same ominous quality in the air that had preceded the awful demonstrations of the Moving Mountain the day before.

There were queer little rumbling noises within the heart of the mountain, and at times the earth quivered beneath their feet so that they had hard work to maintain their balance.

"I'll bet we have another earthquake before this day is done," muttered Frank uneasily.

Bomba said nothing. His mind was intent on Jojasta. Was the man himself as terrible as the place in which he dwelt? If so, it boded ill for the success of his mission.

Suddenly a cry of surprise came from Frank's lips, and he pointed at something that gleamed white through the wooded slopes of the mountain.

"What's that, Bomba?" he cried. "It's a house of some sort, or——"

"The house of Jojasta!" cried Bomba. "Come!"

His heart was on fire with eagerness, with fear, and with hope. He had nearly reached the end of his journey! His goal was in sight!

In a few moments he and his companion reached a point of vantage, and, concealed behind adjoining trees, gazed with breathless interest on the scene before them.

Dug into the side of the mountain was a level space of considerable extent, made there probably by some convulsion of nature centuries before.

In this space was a great building of white stone that seemed to be half-palace, half-temple There had been walls once, but these had fallen into ruin, and all that remained was the roof supported by colossal pillars of stone. These columns were covered with huge, grotesque figures, half-animal, half-human, carved by hands long since dust.

The eyes of Frank Parkhurst gleamed, for he knew, what Bomba could not, that he was gazing upon the ruins of a building belonging to a civilization so ancient that only a few scattered memorials remained.

After one quick glance at the temple, Bomba's

eyes leaped to a scene of far more poignant interest to him.

Out from the wooded slopes beside the temple there stepped a man. He walked on embroidered sandals and wore a priestly robe of some rich material that hung from his shoulders and was girdled at the waist with a belt that glittered with what seemed to be precious stones.

In his hand he carried a lash of knotted rope. Before him cringed two slaves. On their feet were stone sandals, so heavy that they could scarcely move in them.

Across their bowed and bleeding shoulders were the fresh welts of the lash. They stood on the edge of a cliff and could not retreat. Again and again that lash, wielded with ferocity, ate into their flesh. Then their pitiless driver seemed to go mad with rage.

With the ferocious cry of a jungle beast, he rushed upon the cowering slaves and with a heave of his powerful shoulders pushed them over the cliff!

CHAPTER XX

BURIED ALIVE

WITH horrified cries Bomba and Frank Park-hurst sprang to their feet, staring at the spot where a moment before the slaves had been and trying to trace their downward course.

Then they looked for the cruel taskmaster, but he had mysteriously disappeared.

The boys looked at each other with horror in their eyes.

"Could that have been Jojasta?" asked Frank.

"It must have been," replied Bomba. "He has all power here. Ruspak told me that he did what it pleased him to do, and that none could stand before him."

Bomba was horrified at the ferocity of the man. Could such a demon as that be his father?

"No, no!" he exclaimed passionately. "His heart is black! He is not my father!"

"Look here!" called Frank, who had flung himself face down near the edge of the cliff and was peering over.

Bomba went swiftly toward him.

"There are the slaves!" cried Frank, extending a pointing finger. "They have been caught in the bushes growing out from the side of the mountain."

He had hardly spoken when there was a terrible grumbling in the heart of the moutain that swelled into a roar. Beneath them the ground quivered, undulating with a sickening motion.

"The slaves!" cried Bomba hoarsely. "Look! The ground has opened and swallowed them up. They are gone!"

It was true. Beneath the unfortunate slaves, caught as they were in the tangled bushes, a great hole had opened suddenly in the side of the mountain.

Before the eyes of the horrified boys, dirt, stones and bushes loosed their hold on the earth and slid downward with a terrific roar, bearing the two hapless men with them into that yawning hole.

The earth closed again. It was as though the slaves had never been, so completely had their persons been removed from the face of the earth.

The next moment, Bomba and Frank, standing there spellbound by the awfulness of the tragedy, were deafened by a hideous roar that thrilled them with terror.

Behind them the mountain belched forth a

sheet of flame. The boys started to run, and as they did so the rock and earth beneath their feet gave way. They felt themselves flung out into space, their arms and legs going like windmills, reaching out wildly to clutch anything within reach.

Then they were falling between two walls of rock, from which bushes protruded, breaking their fall to some extent but not stopping it altogether, until they brought up in a mass of brush and branches.

Bomba heard a thud, and the next moment he himself came in contact with something hard, the shock seeming to push his spine up through the top of his head.

He was in darkness—utter, impenetrable darkness. Every bone and muscle in him felt bruised and sore. He sat for a moment, regaining his breath, trying to find in the darkness some faint ray of light.

He thought of his companion? Where was he?

"Frank!" he called, his voice sounding muffled and faint. "Where are you?"

"Here," came an answer, and Bomba could have shouted with joy to find that at least his companion was still alive.

"I will come to you," he said, and began groping his way cautiously toward the sound of the voice.

Frank called out again, and thus aided, Bomba's outstretched hand finally found him.

"This is a fine mess we're in, I'll tell the world," said Frank, as his hand met Bomba's and gripped it. "Where are we, do you suppose? In the middle of the earth?"

"I do not know how deep the earth is," said Bomba, with his usual literalness, "and so I cannot tell if we are in the middle. But I am sure we are somewhere in the Moving Mountain."

Frank groaned.

"Buried alive! We'll never get out of this, Bomba!"

"We will try," said the jungle lad simply.

The calm courage in Bomba's voice roused a faint hope in the mind of the other lad.

"Do you think there is a chance of getting out?" he asked.

For answer Bomba asked a question in his turn.

"Look straight before you, far away," he said. "Do you see a small, red light?"

There was a pause, during which Frank looked long and earnestly.

"I can't say that I do," he said then reluctantly.

"But the eyes of Bomba are used to the dark," the jungle lad persisted. "There is a red glow, but it is far away. But if I can see it, there must be a path that leads to it."

"Then you think there may be a way out?" Frank asked eagerly.

"There may be," said Bomba. "But we must be careful," he added, as Frank got to his feet and started to grope his way forward. "There will be other dangers. Perhaps there will be open places in the road. We must creep forward carefully, like the puma when he smells a trap."

Bomba dropped to hands and knees, and his companion followed suit.

It was well for Bomba that he was cautious. They had gone only a short distance when his hand, groping along the path ahead of him, grasped empty air.

It was another hole, possibly as deep as the one into which they had already fallen.

"Stop where you are," he warned Frank, who was following him closely. "There is danger."

The two boys explored the edge of the hole with great caution. If it did not extend the full width of the tunnel they were exploring, they could circle it and proceed on their journey.

But to their dismay it did extend straight across the tunnel, with the exception of a slight ledge four or five inches wide at one end. But this had been cracked, probably by the earthquake, and pieces of it crumbled in Bomba's hand as he felt of it.

No hope there!

"I guess we're done, Bomba, old boy," said Frank lugubriously. "We shall have to stay here buried in the heart of the earth until we starve to death or die of thirst."

"I am young like you, I am not an 'old boy' like Casson. We can endure. But there is one chance left," said Bomba. "Do you remember, Frank, that you knocked against something big and round just before we got to the hole?"

"I know it nearly cracked my head," replied Frank. "I sure got a peach of a rap."

"That was part of the trunk of a small tree," said Bomba, wondering for a moment what Frank's words meant, but putting aside thought of this that he might give his whole mind to the present. "I felt of it and I know. I think it may be big enough to go across this hole."

Frank caught the idea.

"You mean that the tree will make a bridge that we can walk across?" he asked.

"Yes, if the hole is not too wide for the trunk to reach to the other end," replied Bomba. "We will bring it and try. It is the only chance we have."

Frank was a lad of more than ordinary courage, and was seldom afraid to take a chance.

But to make his way in utter darkness across a chasm of unknown depth on the narrow and slippery trunk of a tree, where the slightest mishap might mean plunging through space to death, was a supreme test of courage.

To Bomba, who was accustomed to the tree bridges of the jungle, the feat was a comparatively simple one, even in the darkness, and he faced it without trepidation.

Frank braced himself. He saw that to follow Bomba's suggestion offered the only chance they had of escape. To stay where they were meant death by starvation, even if, in the meantime, the malevolent Moving Mountain should not again awake to wrath and bury them beneath tons of débris.

"Come!" said Bomba encouragingly. "We will try it, and then we will see what that red glow means."

"Probably leads to another of the Caves of Fire," muttered Frank, who was in anything but an optimistic mood. "But I'm game. Lead on, Bomba."

The jungle boy led the way back to the segment of tree trunk that had probably been engulfed from the upper air in some one of the convulsions of the mountain.

They found it and rolled it near the edge of the hole. Then by their joint exertions they stood it

on end and pushed it so that it fell over toward
the further side of the chasm.

Would the end of the trunk find a lodgment on
the further side? Or was the hole so wide that
the trunk would not span it but itself drop into the
chasm?

They held their breath as they awaited the
answer to the question on which their lives depended.

There was a heavy thud as the further end of
the trunk found a resting place. They had made
their bridge!

Frank squared his shoulders and summoned up
all his resolution. He would show the boy from
the jungle that he was not afraid, that he could
face danger with as high a courage as anyone
could show.

"You go first," said Bomba. "I will be close
behind you, touching you, and if you fall, I will
catch you. The hole is not wide. We shall soon
be across."

Frank drew a long breath and stepped out on
the tree trunk. He slipped, and Bomba drew him
quickly back.

"Take off those things from your feet," directed Bomba. "I should have told you before.
You must have bare feet or you cannot cross."

Frank fumbled with straps and buckles and
finally kicked off the heavy jungle boots.

"Do not leave them behind," counseled Bomba. "You will need them after we get across."

Frank did as directed, and Bomba, who himself had slipped off his sandals, preceded him this time on their improvised bridge.

"It may be best for me to go first, after all," he said. "You hold on to me and you will be safe. For Bomba has crossed angry waters on only the trunk of a tree."

So Frank put one hand on the bare brown shoulder of Bomba, and, balancing himself with the other, followed his guide.

Bomba went slowly, placing each foot with the utmost care. If only there had been light, the faintest glimmer of light, to show him what lay ahead!

Frank came close behind him, trying to dig his bare toes into the slippery, treacherous bark of the tree. He felt like a tight-rope walker crossing a perilous chasm. Each step he took he felt might be the last.

He felt dizzy, weak. It was only by the greatest effort of his will that he forced himself to stand upright, to go forward step by step.

There was a curious sinking movement of the bridge. The trunk, though it had reached the other side, must have fallen on the very edge of the chasm, and under their weight and movement was slipping off the brink.

Frank could feel himself slowly sinking with the log.

"Bomba!" he cried despairingly. "I'm going! Help me!"

He felt his upflung arm grasped in fingers of steel.

"I'm on land," gasped Bomba from somewhere in the darkness above him. "I'll hold on to you. Try to climb up to me. I——"

The sentence was not finished, but Frank could feel that Bomba, too, was slipping—slipping into that awful abyss that yawned beneath them!

CHAPTER XXI

IN THE DEPTHS

JUST as Frank felt that his doom was sealed, his descent was suddenly stopped.

For Bomba, at the moment when he had been pulled by Frank's sudden weight almost halfway over the brink of the chasm, had found a toehold in a cleft of rock.

He held on to it with the strength of desperation. The log had fallen now, and Frank was swinging in mid-air, his entire weight on Bomba's arms.

Inch by inch, straining to the utmost, Bomba pulled himself back, bringing Frank along with him until the latter got his elbows on the ledge and thus relieved the jungle lad of some of the strain. Then, with one last tremendous tug, Bomba drew the yellow-haired lad up over the edge and on to solid ground.

Only the awful need of the moment had given Bomba the superhuman strength needed for the task. And when at last it was accomplished he lay back on the ground limp and exhausted.

For a time neither of the boys spoke.

Then Frank touched Bomba on the arm and said with a voice full of emotion:

"That's the second time you've saved my life. Bomba, you're the finest fellow alive! And what strength you have! Your muscles must be made of iron."

"I could not let you fall," replied Bomba. "I told your mother I would bring you back to her. Bomba must keep his word."

"You're a brick!" said Frank. "I wish you were my brother."

"So do I," said Bomba, stirred to the depths by his companion's last words.

He was delighted beyond measure that he had saved Frank's life, for already he had grown fond of the youth. But, in addition to this, he had an intense satisfaction in feeling that he had acted as a white boy should. His soul as well as his skin demonstrated his kinship with the whites! Now the woman with the golden hair would be sure that he was not a native!

Frank looked over the edge of the chasm and shuddered.

"That must be frightfully deep," he said. "It was a long time before I heard the log crash at the bottom."

"Yes," agreed Bomba. "But now we must be going on."

He rose to his feet, and Frank followed his example, although his legs felt very shaky under him.

Their progress was necessarily slow, because there was always the danger of encountering another hole like that from which they had so narrowly escaped.

The road had no further break in it, however, and in a little while they had drawn perceptibly nearer to the light that had been detected by the keen eyes of Bomba. But, as the light became more pronounced, the atmosphere grew hotter until their clothes were drenched with perspiration and their lips and tongues were parched.

Soon they could detect that the light was caused by thin streaks of flame and their hearts sank beneath them. Even if an opening to the outer air lay behind those flames, they could never run that fiery gantlet.

The heat at last became so unbearable that they were forced to come to a halt. Already their flesh was almost blistering.

"This mountain must be a volcano," declared Frank, in accents of despair. "There seems to be fire wherever we go."

"What is a volcano?" asked Bomba, who had never heard the word.

"It's a mountain that throws out flame and ashes and melted rock that they call lava," replied Frank. "Every once in a while it goes on a spree and sends everything that's in it up toward the sky. And when it does this next time, it's a good bet that we'll be thrown out with the rest."

It looked indeed as though the boys had come to the end of their resources. They could not go back because of the chasm. They could not go forward because of the fire.

In addition, they were wolfishly hungry, as they had not eaten for hours, and their thirst was intolerable. They had not a scrap of food or a drop of water with them, as they had counted on securing these while on their journey.

"I'd give a million dollars, if I had it, for a drink of water," groaned Frank.

"We will find some yet," said Bomba, whose indomitable courage refused to quail. "We will —what was that?"

He stood rigid in a listening attitude.

"What is it?" asked Frank, with a sudden renewal of hope.

"I hear men talking," said Bomba. "Do not speak. I must find out where the words come from."

Frank became mute.

"It is over this way," said Bomba finally pointing to the right. "They are talking, and they are in trouble. We will see if there is a road that leads to them."

With his hands he felt along the sides of the tunnel, and in a few minutes an exclamation of satisfaction came from him.

"It is here," he said. "Come! Stay close to me and keep your hand on my shoulder."

He led the way into an opening so narrow that the boys could touch the walls on each side and so low that they had to proceed in a stooping position.

As they advanced, the voices grew clearer to Bomba's ears, and soon Frank himself heard them. They could not catch the meaning, but they knew that they were human sounds.

In their forlorn condition this cheered them immeasurably and they were delighted to note, too, that the way was getting lighter, not with the rosy light that betokened fire but with a white light that indicated some connection with the outside world. It was very dim, but enormously welcome after the darkness that had engulfed them.

At a turning in the passage they came upon a mass of branches and débris, entangled in which and struggling to free themselves they could faintly discern two figures.

From a great distance above a few rays of light came from some unseen opening.

The truth burst upon Bomba.

"They are the slaves!" he cried. "The men who were pushed over the side of the mountain by Jojasta. And they are still alive. Come, let us help them."

The boys hurried over to the mass of débris from which the upper part of the men's bodies protruded. A cry broke from the trapped victims as they perceived the lads' approach.

"Help us, masters! Help us!" they begged, in their native tongue.

There was no need to urge. The boys fell to with a will, dragging away the masses of dirt and brush until finally they were able to pull the men out. The latter had been handicapped in their efforts by the heavy stone sandals they wore.

These were held in place by heavy straps and buckles that the boys speedily unloosed and threw to one side.

The gratitude of the rescued slaves was beyond words. They prostrated themselves at their deliverers' feet and broke into incoherent thanks, while tears rolled down their faces.

"You have saved us!" cried one.

"We are yours!" exclaimed the other. "Do with us as you will!"

CHAPTER XXII

THE TEMPLE FALLS

Bomba and Frank were touched and at the
same time embarrassed by the profuse gratitude
of the two unfortunate men.

"It's nice to feel that they'd do anything in the
world for us," murmured Frank to Bomba. "But,
after all, they're in our identical fix, and they
probably can't do one blessed thing to help us."
He had been in the jungle long enough to understand a part of what had been said.

Bomba was not so sure of that. It had struck
him as he had gone along that some of these
passages were too regular to be due to mere
freaks of nature and might perhaps be the work
of human hands.

"Do you know this place?" he asked. "Have
you ever been here before?"

The reply almost took his breath from amazement and delight.

"Yes," answered the one who seemed to be the
more intelligent of the two. "When the earth
caved in and we fell here, we saw that we were in

one of the secret paths that go under the temple of Jojasta. There are many of them."

"Do you know the way that leads out to the open places?" asked Bomba eagerly.

"Yes," was the reply. "Ashati and Neram can guide you to a place where you can see the sun again and have it shine on you."

"What was it he said?" asked Frank, who could see from the expression on Bomba's face that the news the men had given was good. "I didn't quite catch it."

"They know this place," responded Bomba. "These are the secret paths of Jojasta, and the slaves say that they will lead us out to where the sun shines."

"Glory hallelujah!" cried Frank, as he clapped his companion on the shoulder. "And here a minute ago I wouldn't have given a plugged nickel for our chances!"

Bomba turned to the men, who had by this time recovered something of their strength.

"Can you walk now?" he asked, as he looked with pity at the scarred and bleeding backs of the unfortunates.

"Yes," replied Ashati, who seemed to be the spokesman for the two. "We will take you where you will. There is a passage that goes to the white temple of Ro-Lat. But if you go that way, you may meet Jojasta."

"That is what I want to do," replied Bomba. "It is for that that I have come to this place of the Moving Mountain."

The slaves looked at each other in wonder. That anyone in his senses should want to meet Jojosta seemed to them incredible.

"Is he such a bad man?" queried Bomba.

The men looked about them fearfully, as though they thought the walls might have ears.

"He has a black heart," replied Ashati. "He hurts and kills. And he gets more wild and savage with every moon. All tremble before him."

Bomba could well believe this from the scene his own eyes had witnessed. But he was none the less determined to meet the strange medicine man face to face.

"I do not fear the wrath of Jojasta," he said simply. "But what about you? He tried to kill you once, and he may try to kill you again."

The slaves bowed their heads and crossed their hands submissively on their breasts.

"It is as the gods will," said Ashati, and Neram nodded his head in acquiescence.

At a sign from Bomba, they started off in the lead, threading the passageways with an assurance that told of their perfect familiarity with the place.

As they advanced, the light grew gradually brighter, and before long they had reached the bottom of a shaft, looking up which the boys could catch a glimpse of the sky.

Frank fairly danced with delight, and Bomba, though more self-contained, shared in his companion's joy.

"Good old daylight!" cried Frank. "I never expected to see you again."

At the foot of the shaft was a little platform from which a spiral staircase of stone steps wound upward. A little off to the right was a stone basin, half filled with water.

Before doing anything else, the boys rushed to this and drank their fill. Then they dashed some of it over their heated faces, and felt refreshed beyond measure.

Just as they were preparing to ascend the steps, a deep, growling sound came to their ears, and the rock beneath their feet was shaken violently.

"What's that?" demanded Frank.

"Quick!" said Ashati. "The mountain is beginning to move. Perhaps Jojasta knows we are here and is calling upon the mountain to bury us alive."

"Come!" cried the jungle boy.

With a bound Bomba was on the lower step of the spiral staircase, with Frank close behind him. The slaves of Jojasta followed, and all began the ascent.

It was a nightmare climb, with everything swaying dizzily about them, the staircase itself shaking as if it would throw them off. It would have done so at times, if they had not dropped to their hands and knees and hung on to the rough stone for dear life.

As they neared the top they could hear cries of terror and the rush of flying feet, and when at last they stepped out on the platform of the temple, they were almost knocked off their feet by the crowd of natives running past them, as from some dire threatened calamity.

A glance around was sufficient to explain the fright of the multitude.

From the summit of the mountain towering over them were issuing great sheets of burning lava that fell on the slopes and was flowing down in a fiery flood, winding along the mountainside like flaming, sinuous serpents, some of the streams coming directly toward the opening from which they had emerged.

But the lava was coming slowly, and it would be some time before it reached the platform.

What had caused the mad stampede that nearly swept them away with it was the danger that threatened the temple itself. It was rocking in the earthquake like a ship in a storm.

"Look, Bomba!" exclaimed Frank, his eyes filled with horror, his breath coming in gasps.

Even as the boys looked, a great section of the

roof gave way and fell with a terrific roar, burying beneath it such of the crowd as had not been able to get from under it. The roar of crashing roof and falling columns was thunderous and struck terror to all hearts.

As they ran toward the further end of the platform, Bomba and Frank caught a glimpse through the columns, on the side of the temple still standing, of the figure of the priest kneeling before an altar.

He was dressed in the same sumptuous robes as when they had seen him first. His back was toward them, and he was going through some religious rite, at times raising his hands on high as though invoking the help of the gods.

"It is Jojasta," said Ashati, in awe-struck tones. "He prays at the Altar of Blue Fire."

Bomba's heart leaped. He forgot for the moment the terrors of the earthquake. Here, only a few feet distant, was the man he had come so many miles and dared so many dangers to talk with.

Oblivious of all else, Bomba left his companions and moved across the temple floor toward the kneeling figure.

"Come back!" cried Frank in consternation. "The roof may fall! You will be killed! Come back!"

Bomba made no answer and kept on.

He was nearing the altar when the medicine man rose to his feet. He turned about and his eyes met Bomba's. Ferocity at the intrusion leaped into his eyes, to be replaced almost instantly by a look of wonder and terror. He staggered back.

"Ha! Bartow! Whence do you come?" he screamed, and fell senseless to the floor.

CHAPTER XXIII

THE JAWS OF DEATH

BOMBA leaped forward to lift the stricken man from the floor of the temple.

But even as he stooped, there was a deafening crash and one of the columns of the temple fell within ten feet of him, some of the flying fragments of stone grazing his temple and temporarily stunning him.

As he staggered and would have fallen, he felt himself grasped on either side by strong arms that dragged him out on the open platform from beneath the sagging roof.

When the momentary dizziness had passed and his mind cleared, he was being hurried down a slope of the mountain, with Frank supporting him on one side and Ashati on the other, while Neram followed at their heels.

"That was an awfully close shave!" panted Frank. "A little more and that column would have crushed the life out of you. It's up to us to get away from here while the going's good."

"But Jojasta!" exclaimed Bomba. "I must get

back to him! I must get him out of the ruins! I do not want him to die! I want him to tell me of my father and mother!"

"If you get back to him, you'll have to do it later," said Frank grimly, as he pointed back to a stream of lava that was already flowing between them and the temple platform. "There's no getting past that."

Bomba saw that Frank was right, and with bitter regret he was forced to relinquish his plan for the present, though none the less determined to go back when conditions permitted. It was a terrible disappointment to be halted as he had been just when Jojasta had seemed to be on the brink of a revelation.

But for the moment they had all they could do to provide for their own safety. Ashes and hot stones were falling all about them. They were retarded in their flight by the multitude of fugitives among whom they found themselves. Some were carrying children, others their meager belongings. All were wild-eyed with terror, crazed with desire to get as far away from the scene of eruption as possible.

Ashati and Neram kept close to the boys, for which the latter were grateful, for the slaves, who knew the country thoroughly, could guide them along the best trails. In a little while they had drawn clear of the crowds, and before long they

were out of the zone of the volcano's greatest
activity.

They were pretty well winded when at last
they stopped before an abandoned hut on the
slope of a neighboring hill, to which the two
slaves led them. They entered with a sigh of
relief and threw themselves on the floor, panting
and almost exhausted.

While they were resting, the slaves slipped
out into the jungle and returned before long with
jaboty eggs and fruit and water, of which the
boys partook ravenously. It was not a sumptuous
meal, but even to Frank, in his famished condition, it was a royal feast.

"Tell me, Ashati," said Bomba, when the meal
was finished. "Did you ever hear the name of
Bartow?"

The slave shook his head in the negative.

"Or Laura?" persisted Bomba.

"No," said Ashati.

"How long has Jojasta been the ruler here?"
asked Bomba.

"For many years," replied Ashati. "I do not
know how many. My father was his slave before
I was born."

"Do you remember that he ever had a white
wife?" asked Bomba.

"Yes," said Ashati. "She was very beautiful.
She was saved alive when a camp of her people

was raided and all the others killed. Jojasta made her his wife. But she was not happy, and after her son was born she went with him into the Caves of Fires. Some thought she had wandered there without knowing what they were and was lost. Others said that she was glad to go there to end her life. But this they said in whispers, for fear it might come to the ears of Jojasta."

"Do you think I look like her or like Jojasta?" asked Bomba.

Ashati studied him keenly.

"You are different from Jojasta," he declared. "As for the woman, it was many years ago and I do not remember well. But I do not think you are like her. Her eyes were the color of the sky and her hair was of gold. Your eyes and hair are the color of muddy water. No, you do not look as she did. But you are not like Jojasta."

Although this was far from conclusive, it served to confirm Bomba's growing conviction that Jojasta was not his father. And he was glad of this, for the ruthless brutality of the man had filled him with repulsion.

But Jojasta knew Bartow. And what was more, he feared him. Else why the manifest terror in the old medicine man's eyes and the swoon that had sent him to the floor?

And he had thought that Bomba was Bartow.

The only inference that could be drawn from this was that he, Bomba, was the son of Bartow. That, if true, was something. But it was far from being enough. It simplified the problem, but by no means solved it.

He would try to reach Jojasta on the morrow, as soon as the volcano had spent its fury. Until then, he would have to possess his soul in patience.

In the interval of waiting, he and Frank had their first real chance to get acquainted. And the more they learned of each other the closer they were drawn together.

Bomba listened with wondering eyes as Frank told of the great world without, that so far had been a sealed book to Bomba. For the first time, the jungle lad learned of great oceans studded with ships, of mighty cities with as many people as there were trees in the jungle, of great guns that could send missiles as heavy as a boulder a distance of twenty miles, of lights that started into being like thousands of fireflies on simply pressing a button, of giant buildings, hundreds of feet in height, that towered into the skies, of railroads and telephones, of phonographs and radio and the host of things that make up civilization.

Much of it he could not understand, but all of it he believed. It sounded incredible. It was like witchcraft. But he felt sure that his companion was telling him the truth.

In his turn he told the city boy tales of the jungle that almost made the latter's hair stand on end—the way he had trapped the cooanaradi when the latter had pursued him; how he had tricked the jaguars who had attacked the camp of Gillis and Dorn; his impaling of the jaracara on the spiked branches of the tree; the way he had beaten off the headhunters who had attacked the cabin; his swim for life when the alligator had pursued him; the fight with the vultures; the knifing in the forest of the two Indians who had captured Frank's mother; the capture of Ruspak, the medicine man; the battle with the anaconda in the ygapo.

He told of these things simply, without the slightest trace of boasting. To him they were the inevitable incidents of life in the jungle, but Frank's nerves were tingling with excitement and his eyes glowed with admiration as he listened.

"Gee, how I wish I'd done the things you've done!" he exclaimed.

"And I wish I could have seen the things you've seen," replied Bomba.

"You will some day," prophesied Frank.

At these words a wild surge of longing thrilled through the jungle boy. Oh, if that prophecy should ever come true! He longed for it with all his heart. It was his right. He was being cheated of his heritage. He was white, as white as Frank himself, and his place was with the whites, his brothers by blood and race.

The two boys were so exhausted by the stirring adventures of the day that they slept soundly that night, despite the rocking of the earth and the roar of the volcano.

When they woke in the morning the tumult had ceased. The wrath of the Moving Mountain had been expended for the present. The sun shone brightly from the azure sky, and all nature was at peace.

"Now I go to find Jojasta, if he is still alive," declared Bomba, after they had finished the hearty breakfast that Ashati and Neram had provided.

Frank did not seek to dissuade him. He knew it would have been useless if he had. So he accompanied his newly made friend, the two rescued slaves following.

The difficulties of the way were many. On every side were evidences of the frightful havoc wrought by the eruption and the earthquake. Bodies of natives were scattered here and there, engulfed by the lava floods before they could escape. The earth was uptorn, and thrown into all sorts of ghastly and fantastic shapes. Trees had been uprooted by the score and barred their way. The lava had ceased to flow, and now lay smoking and hardening beneath the rays of the sun.

With infinite pains and many detours, they finally reached the platform of the temple. Here the desolation was complete. Most of the columns had fallen, and only a few remaining ones upheld a small segment of the temple roof.

They picked their way with care amid the débris. A moment more, and Bomba's keen eyes were rewarded. He rushed toward one of the fallen pillars.

"Here he is!" he cried.

CHAPTER XXIV

WHAT JOJASTA TOLD

FRANK and the two Indians followed Bomba as rapidly as they could, and found him standing at a column beneath which lay Jojasta, the dreaded medicine man of the Moving Mountain.

He lay on his back, near the altar from which he had just risen when Bomba had first come upon him. One of the fallen pillars of the temple lay over his legs, pinning him down.

His swarthy face was livid with pain. It was a powerful face, such as marks a master of men. Deep lines were graven on it that betokened indomitable will and resolution. Ruthlessness, too, was in evidence. It was plain that he was one who would sweep away anything that stood in the way of his settled purpose. And there were signs of intellectual power in the broad forehead that bulged slightly at the temples.

His eyes were closed, but the rising and falling of his chest showed that he still lived.

The first impulse of the newcomers was to pull away the column that had crushed the man's legs.

They tugged at it, but it weighed many tons and they might as well have tried to move a mountain. Death alone could free Jojasta.

As Bomba and his companions realized this, they desisted from their efforts and gathered about the man with pity in their eyes. Even Ashati and Neram, who had no reason to love their cruel taskmaster, were affected by his plight.

As though he were conscious of their scrutiny, Jojasta opened his eyes. He looked around bewilderedly for a moment. Then his gaze fell on Bomba.

A feeble exclamation came from his lips and he made a motion as though he would rise to his feet. Then he realized his condition, and sank back with a groan.

He covered his eyes with his hand, as though to shut out the sight of the jungle lad.

"Bartow!" he muttered. "Why have you come here? Why have you returned to call me to account?"

"I am not Bartow," said Bomba gently. "I have no wish to do you harm. It is you who will tell me about Bartow."

He put his arm under the medicine man's broad shoulders and raised him to a sitting position.

"Get water!" he ordered Neram, and the latter disappeared, to return in a moment with water in one of the ceremonial chalices belonging to the temple.

Bomba put it to Jojasta's lips, and the latter drank it with avidity. Then the lad bathed the man's face, and the refreshment afforded seemed to give a temporary increase of strength to the stricken priest.

"I have come a long way to ask you a question," said Bomba, after a moment.

"Ask it quickly," murmured Jojasta, "for I have not long to live. It is the will of the King of the Sky."

"Tell me," asked Bomba, his voice vibrant with emotion. "Are you my father?"

"No, no!" cried Jojasta, with a surprise and energy in his voice that carried conviction.

"Then your white wife was not named Laura?" went on Bomba.

"No! Why do you ask?" returned Jojasta, after a moment's pause.

"Do you know of any woman with the name of Laura?" persisted Bomba.

A look of stubbornness, with an admixture of cunning, came into Jojasta's eyes, and he remained mute.

"Do you?" repeated Bomba.

"There are some things that are not permitted to be told," was the reply.

"I must know the names of my father and

mother," said Bomba, determination in his voice. "Who are they? Who am I?"

"Who are you?" repeated Jojasta, with a flash of his old energy. "Who? Ask Bartow. Ask Sobrinini."

"Who are they?" pleaded Bomba.

"What? Know you not Sobrinini of the Pilati tribe, they who dwell in sight of the Giant Cataract over by the setting sun? Ask her! Ask her who Bartow is, where Bartow is. Sobrinini can tell you!"

"Can Sobrinini tell me of Laura, too? If I find Bartow, shall I find Laura?" demanded Bomba, wrought up and excited.

"But you are Bartow!" Jojasta shrieked. "If you are not Bartow, you are his ghost!"

The outburst exhausted Jojasta's fast waning strength, and he fell back unconscious.

Bomba again bathed his hands and face and sought desperately to revive him, but in vain.

Just then there came a thunderous roar and the floor shook so violently under Bomba that he was thrown headlong.

He tried to get to his feet, and was again flung down, at the same time that some of the remaining pillars came down with a fearful crash.

"Quick, Bomba, run!" shouted Frank. "The platform is sinking. Come! Quick!"

Bomba felt the floor giving way beneath him.

He made a jump and just barely reached the ground.

Then, with a terrific roar, the ground beneath the platform opened, and down into the yawning abyss went the whole structure, roof, pillars, platform, in one wild welter of ruin, carrying Jojasta to his doom!

CHAPTER XXV

BOMBA KEEPS HIS PROMISE

THE catastrophe was appalling and filled Bomba and Frank with horror.

But they had little time to dwell upon it then. Death, in one of its most terrible forms, threatened them.

The earth surged like the sea. All nature was in the throes of a mighty convulsion. Trees were falling all about them. From the peak of the Moving Mountain great streams of liquid fire shot up into the sky, some of the spray falling so near them that their flesh was blistered by the drops.

Stumbling, sliding, falling, the boys and the natives made their way down the mountain slope, avoiding with difficulty the many entrances to the Caves of Fire, from which tongues of flame were darting forth and trying to envelop them.

They did not stop this time at the hut in which they had passed the night, for that, too, was in the earthquake zone, which seemed to have widened. All their energies were bent on getting away with the greatest possible speed from that horrible scene of death and destruction.

On they went, panting, gasping, rushing headlong, stumbling. On and on, through valleys and over hills, until finally they reached a ridge where the ground no longer shook. There they threw themselves upon the ground and lay for a long time recovering their breath, no one of them able to say a word.

But if their tongues were silent, their eyes were busy. From where they lay the Moving Mountain was in full sight. The summit was enveloped in smoke, through which tore great streaks of flame like jagged arrows of lightning.

As they looked, they could see that the mountain was justifying its name. It was moving, slowly, majestically, but undeniably moving, as though it were endued with life.

To the onlookers, however, it was more significant of death. They shuddered as they remembered their narrow escapes of the last few days. There had been moments when their lives had not seemed worth a moment's purchase. But, though wounded and bruised, they had escaped alive.

Frank was the first to break the silence.

"I came into the jungle to have adventure," he said. "And I sure got more than I bargained for. I've had enough crowded into the last few days to last me for the rest of my life. I'm no hog, and I know when I have enough! It's me now for the camp and then for the coast. What do you say, Bomba, to making tracks? I suppose you haven't any reason to stay about here any longer."

"No," agreed Bomba slowly. "We will go. I have seen Jojasta. He did not tell me all I wanted, but he told me something. He thought I was Bartow when he saw me. If I am so much like him, it must be that Bartow is my father. I am glad that Jojasta was not my father, for he was a man of blood."

"Why do you suppose he refused to answer when you asked him about Laura?" queried Frank curiously.

"That I do not know," replied Bomba sadly. "He knew something, but he would not tell. I shall have to go to the one he called Sobrinini and find out what she knows."

"But there will be a good deal of risk about that, won't there?" asked Frank. "You know that's somewhere near the Giant Cataract, where-ever that is, and it's there you told me that the headhunters lived. They'll have it in for you after what you've done to them."

"Have it in for me?"

"They will be your enemies," explained Frank.

"There will be danger," admitted Bomba. "But I will go just the same. But first I must get back to Casson. My heart is sore and heavy for him, for I do not know whether he is dead or alive. I will take you to your camp, as I promised the woman with the golden hair I would do. Then I will go to Casson. After that to Sobrinini. Come, let us go."

"Your slaves whom you saved will follow," said Ashati.

"No, Ashati," replied Bomba. "Stay with your own people. The other Indians will not give you welcome, and you will be alone and unhappy. Come, Frank."

They rose to their feet, while Ashati and Neram watched them wistfully. They had become attached to the young lads, the first probably who had shown pity for them in all their lives, and they were sad at the thought of parting.

"We are sorry to leave you," said Bomba, as he patted them in a friendly way on their shoulders. "We have helped you, and you have helped us. Your hearts are good. And it is well for your sakes that Jojasta is dead."

"Yes; and for the others of the tribe," replied Ashati. "All hated him, while they feared him. Now there will be a new medicine man, and things may be better with our people. May the young masters have good fortune as they go home through the jungle. They have been good to us."

There was a warm leavetaking, and with a

parting wave of the hand the boys plunged into the jungle.

They traveled rapidly, and, thanks to Bomba's marvelous sense of direction, in almost a beeline to the camp.

As the boys approached its vicinity, their hearts were in a tremor from different emotions. Frank was eager for the embrace of his mother and wild with anxiety about his father. Bomba was exultant in the thought that he had kept his promise to the woman with hair like the sun. She had trusted him, and he had not failed her.

She was the first they saw when they broke through the fringe of trees that edged the clearing where the camp was set up. Her back was to them, and she was busily engaged on some camp task.

"Mother!" cried Frank, as he made a rush toward her.

The woman turned with an exclamation of surprise and joy, and the next moment mother and son were in each others' arms.

Two men came running out at the commotion, one of whom Bomba recognized as Mrs. Parkhurst's brother, Gerald Hicks. As to the identity of the other there was no doubt, for he ran to the mother and son, threw his arms about them, and, strong man as he was, mingled his tears of joy and theirs.

"My son! My dear boy!" he cried. "Oh, you are alive!"

Bomba hung about uneasily, strongly moved by the scene of reunion, and to his surprise found his own eyes full of tears. No father had ever flung his arms about him. No mother had ever kissed him tenderly.

The first ecstasy of reunion passed, Mrs. Parkhurst caught sight of Bomba. She ran toward him, folded him in her arms and rained kisses on his face.

"You dear boy! You brave boy!" she sobbed. "You've brought my son to me! Oh, you are wonderful!"

A moment later Mr. Parkhurst had the lad's hand in his and threw his arm about his shoulders.

"You saved my wife's life, and now you have brought our son to us," he said in husky tones. "How can I ever thank you enough?"

Frank's uncle was not behind the others in gratitude and admiration. And that admiration grew ever greater as Frank, when they had all quieted down a little, told of the way the jungle lad had met almost insuperable difficulties, conquered them, and brought him in safety to the camp.

Mr. Parkhurst, it developed, had eluded the pursuit of the Indians, and after days of wandering in the jungle had been found by a friendly native and brought to camp.

They had a royal feast that night, and Bomba was the guest of honor. All of them were eager to have him go back with them to civilization. The Parkhursts promised to adopt him, educate him, and provide for his future.

The offer was very alluring, and it cost Bomba a pang to refuse it. His imagination had been stirred by Frank's description of the wonders of civilized life, and he longed beyond expression to go with them.

But despite the urge within him, he was adamant. There was Casson. He could not leave him. And there was the mystery about his parentage. He must solve it before he left the jungle.

Though greatly disappointed, the others admired Bomba's loyalty, and after a time forebore to press him. But they did exact a pledge from him that as soon as his work was done he would get in touch with them through the Apex Rubber Corporation on the coast.

He stayed at the camp that night, but at dawn, followed by thanks and blessings and with a last kiss from Mrs. Parkhurst on his lips, waved his new friends farewell and set out through the jungle.

He traveled fast, for he was anxious to get back to the old naturalist. He would stay with

Casson a while, provide for his wants, and then set out on his journey to Sobrinini.

What desperate perils and thrilling adventures he met with on that quest will be told in the next book of this series, entitled: "Bomba the Jungle Boy at the Giant Cataract; or, Chief Nascanora and His Captives."

Bomba was very thoughtful as he threaded his way through the jungle. In his heart was a tumult of emotions. On his lips still lingered the kiss of the woman with the golden hair.

"What must it be to have a mother like that?" he asked his starved and lonely heart. Or a father like the stalwart, handsome man who had pressed Frank to his heart?

Would he ever know? Would he ever find Bartow and Laura? Would he ever take his place where he belonged, a white boy among white people? His heart ached with longing.

To ease the ache a little, he took his harmonica from his pouch and put it to his lips. As the plaintive strains echoed through the forest, he became conscious from the rustling in the trees that his friends were coming.

Kiki and Woowoo, the parrots, fluttered to perches on his shoulders. Doto, the monkey, dropped from branches and gamboled about, wild with joy at his return. Other furred and feathered things joined him and accompanied him.

They loved him. They trusted him. His heart warmed toward them.

"You are my friends," he said, as he petted and caressed each in turn. "Bomba is glad to see you again. But he cannot stay with you long. For he must go to Sobrinini, who can tell him what he wants to know. And after that he may go where there are oceans and ships and cities and many great and wonderful things. The people there have white skins and their souls are awake. Bomba belongs there and must go there. They are his people. For Bomba's skin is white, and even if his soul is not awake, it is waking!"

THE END

THE GREAT ACE SERIES

By NOËL SAINSBURY, JR.

Author of THE CHAMPION SPORT STORIES

*12mo. Cloth. Illustrated. Jacket in colors.
Price 50 cents per volume. Postage 10
cents additional.*

*Here is a series of rattling good flying
stories told by an expert. A boy-aviator's
adventures in the wilds of New Guinea,
Arabia, South America and other strange
lands. Billy Smith, son of an eminent
explorer, learns to pilot a seaplane aboard
a Naval Air Station, and immediately
fares forth upon a series of the most exciting cruises and mysterious quests by
air, by land and by sea that have ever
fallen to the lot of man. The author, a
traveller and ex-naval aviator, brings
many of his own adventures into these tales. Every boy with a drop
of red blood in his veins will want to join Billy Smith in his thrilling quests.*

1. BILLY SMITH—EXPLORING ACE
or By Airplane to New Guinea
The story of a fourteen-year-old lad, taught to pilot a seaplane by his
uncle, Lieut.-Commander on a Naval Air Station. Together they are forced
down at sea, and Lieut.-Com. Smith is so impressed with the lad's courage
in this trying situation that he takes Billy with him to New Guinea to help
search for Billy's father.

2. BILLY SMITH—SECRET SERVICE ACE
or Airplane Adventures in Arabia
Billy Smith again proves his mettle in a series of adventures that take
him to Port Sudan on the Red Sea and the Holy City of Hejaz.

3. BILLY SMITH—MYSTERY ACE
or Airplane Discoveries in South America
Doctor Stanton, bird man of the Natural History Museum disappeared
in the Amazon Jungles. The Smiths, father and son are ordered to find him,
and the trail leads to an outpost rubber plantation, where Billy is lost in the
jungle and captured by the cannibal Mangeroma Indians.

4. BILLY SMITH—TRAIL EATER ACE
or Into the Wilds of Northern Alaska
Another exciting story. Billy Smith and his pal, Nuky, with the aid
of Billy's father set a trap to catch desperate gangsters which they succeed
in doing after many thrilling adventures.

5. BILLY SMITH—SHANGHAIED ACE
or Malay Pirates and Solomon Island Cannibals
Billy shanghaied while on a search for a missing steamer and one pas-
senger in particular, escapes in time to be of vast help, after all, and bring
off a famous rescue in the South Sea Islands.

These books may be purchased wherever books are sold
Send for Our Free Illustrated Catalogue

CUPPLES & LEON COMPANY, Publishers   **New York**

MYSTERY AND ADVENTURE
BOOKS FOR BOYS

THE BASEBALL JOE SERIES

By LESTER CHADWICK

12mo. Illustrated. Price 50 cents per volume.
Postage 10 cents additional.

1. **BASEBALL JOE OF THE SILVER STARS**
   or The Rivals of Riverside

2. **BASEBALL JOE ON THE SCHOOL NINE**
   or Pitching for the Blue Banner

3. **BASEBALL JOE AT YALE**
   or Pitching for the College Championship

4. **BASEBALL JOE IN THE CENTRAL LEAGUE**
   or Making Good as a Professional Pitcher

5. **BASEBALL JOE IN THE BIG LEAGUE**
   or A Young Pitcher's Hardest Struggles

6. **BASEBALL JOE ON THE GIANTS**
   or Making Good as a Twirler in the Metropolis

7. **BASEBALL JOE IN THE WORLD SERIES**
   or Pitching for the Championship

8. **BASEBALL JOE AROUND THE WORLD**
   or Pitching on a Grand Tour

9. **BASEBALL JOE: HOME RUN KING**
   or The Greatest Pitcher and Batter on Record

10. **BASEBALL JOE SAVING THE LEAGUE**
    or Breaking Up a Great Conspiracy

11. **BASEBALL JOE CAPTAIN OF THE TEAM**
    or Bitter Struggles on the Diamond

12. **BASEBALL JOE CHAMPION OF THE LEAGUE**
    or The Record that was Worth While

13. **BASEBALL JOE CLUB OWNER**
    or Putting the Home Town on the Map

14. **BASEBALL JOE PITCHING WIZARD**
    or Triumphs Off and On the Diamond

Send for Our Free Illustrated Catalogue.

CUPPLES & LEON COMPANY, Publishers   New York

ADVENTURE STORIES FOR BOYS

By JOHN GABRIEL ROWE

12mo. Cloth. Illustrated. Colored Jacket.
Price 50 cents per volume.
Postage 10 cents additional.

Every boy who knows the lure of exploring and who loves to rig up huts and caves and tree-houses to fortify himself against imaginary enemies will enjoy these books, for they give a vivid chronicle of the doings and inventions of a group of boys who are shipwrecked and have to make themselves snug and safe in tropical islands where the dangers are too real for play.

1. CRUSOE ISLAND
Dick, Alf and Fred find themselves stranded on an unknown island with the old seaman Josh, their ship destroyed by fire, their friends lost.

2. THE ISLAND TREASURE
With much ingenuity these boys fit themselves into the wild life of the island they are cast upon after a storm.

3. THE MYSTERY OF THE DERELICT
Their ship and companions perished in tempest at sea, the boys are adrift in a small open boat when they spy a ship. Such a strange vessel!—no hand guiding it, no soul on board,—a derelict.

4. THE LIGHTSHIP PIRATES
Modern Pirates, with the ferocity of beasts, attack a lightship crew;—recounting the adventures that befall the survivors of that crew—and—"RETRIBUTION."

5. THE SECRET OF THE GOLDEN IDOL
Telling of a mutiny, and how two youngsters were unwillingly involved in one of the weirdest of treasure hunts,—and—"THE GOLDEN FETISH."

6. SERGEANT DICK
The Canadian Northwest police has the reputation of always getting their man, and Sergeant Dick upholds the tradition in a story of great adventure.

7. THE CARCAJOU (kärcájöu)
A sequel to Sergeant Dick, with the Carcajou proving his worth in a series of adventures that will hold the interest of any boy.

These books may be purchased wherever books are sold
Send for Our Free Illustrated Catalogue

CUPPLES & LEON COMPANY, Publishers   New York

THE GREAT MARVEL SERIES

By ROY ROCKWOOD

12mo. Cloth. Illustrated. Jacket in Colors.
Price, per volume, 50 cents.
Postage 10 cents extra.

Since the days of Jules Verne, tales of flying machines and submarine boats have enjoyed increasing popularity. Stories of adventures, in strange places, with peculiar people and queer animals, make this series noteworthy and popular.

1. THROUGH THE AIR TO THE NORTH POLE

The tale of a wonderful cruise to the frozen north and adventures with a degree of reality that is almost convincing.

2. UNDER THE OCEAN TO THE SOUTH POLE

A marvelous trip from Maine to the South Pole, telling of adventures with the sea-monsters and savages.

3. FIVE THOUSAND MILES UNDERGROUND

A cruise to the center of the earth through an immense hole found at an island in the ocean.

4. THROUGH SPACE TO MARS

This book tells how the journey was made in a strange craft and what happened on Mars.

5. LOST ON THE MOON

Strange adventures on the planet which is found to be a land of desolation and silence.

6. ON A TORN-AWAY WORLD

After a tremendous convulsion of nature the adventurers find themselves captives on a vast "island in the air."

7. THE CITY BEYOND THE CLOUDS

The City Beyond the Clouds is a weird place, full of surprises, and the impish Red Dwarfs caused no end of trouble.

8. BY AIR EXPRESS TO VENUS

Our heroes are captured by strange inhabitants of the inside world and have a series of adventures as wonderful as they are absorbing.

Send for Our Free Illustrated Catalogue

CUPPLES & LEON COMPANY, Publishers   New York

THE MOTOR BOYS SERIES

By CLARENCE YOUNG

12mo. Cloth. Illustrated. Jacket in full colors.
Price 50 cents per volume. Postage 10 cents additional.

Bright up-to-date stories, full of information as well as of adventure. Read the first volume and you will want all the others written by Mr. Young.

1. THE MOTOR BOYS
2. THE MOTOR BOYS OVERLAND
3. THE MOTOR BOYS IN MEXICO
4. THE MOTOR BOYS ACROSS THE PLAINS
5. THE MOTOR BOYS AFLOAT
6. THE MOTOR BOYS ON THE ATLANTIC
7. THE MOTOR BOYS IN STRANGE WATERS
8. THE MOTOR BOYS ON THE PACIFIC
9. THE MOTOR BOYS IN THE CLOUDS
10. THE MOTOR BOYS OVER THE ROCKIES
11. THE MOTOR BOYS OVER THE OCEAN
12. THE MOTOR BOYS ON THE WING
13. THE MOTOR BOYS AFTER A FORTUNE
14. THE MOTOR BOYS ON THE BORDER
15. THE MOTOR BOYS UNDER THE SEA
16. THE MOTOR BOYS ON ROAD AND RIVER

Send for Our Free Illustrated Catalogue

CUPPLES & LEON COMPANY, Publishers   New York